Sherlock Holmes These Scattered Houses

An Untold Adventure of the Great Hiatus

As discovered by
Gretchen Altabef

First edition published in 2019
© Copyright 2019
Gretchen Altabef

The right of Gretchen Altabef to be identified as the author of this work has been asserted by her in accordance with the Copyright, Designs and Patents Act 1998.

All rights reserved. No reproduction, copy or transmission of this publication may be made without express prior written permission. No paragraph of this publication may be reproduced, copied or transmitted except with express prior written permission or in accordance with the provisions of the Copyright Act 1956 (as amended). Any person who commits any unauthorised act in relation to this publication may be liable to criminal prosecution and civil claims for damage.

All characters appearing in this work are fictitious. Any resemblance to real persons, living or dead, is purely coincidental. The opinions expressed herein are those of the author and not of MX Publishing.

Paperback ISBN 978-1-78705-487-5
ePub ISBN 978-1-78705-488-2
PDF ISBN 978-1-78705-489-9

Published by MX Publishing
335 Princess Park Manor, Royal Drive,
London, N11 3GX
www.mxpublishing.com

Cover design by Brian Belanger

This book is dedicated to
Michael Altabef

"Good night sweet prince, flights of angels sing thee to thy rest!"
William Shakespeare. "Hamlet." Act 5 Scene 2.

Contents

PROLOGUE..7
CHAPTER 1..18
    A New York Warning
CHAPTER 2..28
    The Science of Strings
CHAPTER 3..33
    Icy Inducements
CHAPTER 4..38
    Auspicious Alliances
CHAPTER 5..42
    A Vassar Tea
CHAPTER 6..49
    A Lady of Rare Character
CHAPTER 7..61
    Houdini's Key
CHAPTER 8..67
    The Story of Mr. Morse
CHAPTER 9..73
    The Rat
CHAPTER 10..77
    A Chain of Events
CHAPTER 11..85
    The Men from Poughkeepsie
CHAPTER 12..91
    A Dawning Light
CHAPTER 13..98
    The Problem

CHAPTER 14..109

    Fixing the Nets
CHAPTER 15..116
    True American Revolutionaries
CHAPTER 16..131
    Two Broken Threads
CHAPTER 17..139
    Great Elemental Forces of Nature
CHAPTER 18..148
    The Darkest Hour
CHAPTER 19..167
    A River of Fear
CHAPTER 20..180
    Mrs. Pinto Vs the Lunacy Commission
CHAPTER 21..184
    The Solution
CHAPTER 22..197
    A Break in the Chain
CHAPTER 23..202
    A Dangerous Retrospection
CHAPTER 24..213
    An Entirely Connected Case
ACKNOWLEDGEMENTS...223
EPILOGUE - FINAL REVEAL......................................225
SELECTED BIBLOGRAPHY...230

Note: This American journal is to be retained until my reappearance in London when I will have joined once again with my dear friend and colleague. Especially as this adventure occurred during the years which followed my much-rumoured demise. If for unforeseen causes I am unable to re-join him, this document is the sole property of Dr. John H. Watson, No. 221B, Baker Street, London, England.

S. H.

PROLOGUE

"...upon his entrance I had instantly recognized the extreme personal danger in which I lay. The only conceivable escape for him lay in silencing my tongue. In an instant I had slipped the revolver from the drawer into my pocket, and was covering him through the cloth. At his remark I drew the weapon out..."–Dr. John H. Watson. "The Adventure of the Final Problem."

Three years as an operative, my hands red with carnage, I resolved to return to London and conclude this protracted sojourn. I kept my horse skirting the mountains as we travelled west to the medieval Italian town of *Riva del Garda*. I dismounted at Hotel Sole at the mouth of the lake and the feet of the Dolomites. Through the *Piazza III Novembre* I stretched my legs with a walk to the *Tabaccheria*. I climbed a series of wide stone stairs, with a high stone wall on one side and straw-grass on the other.

A segment of the stone wall shattered in front of me and I involuntarily fell dead to the hard cold floor, gun in hand. A full-bearded man in a *carabinieri* uniform furtively surveyed the surrounding area and watched me as he walked to the stairs, and kicked me with his boot. I grabbed it, twisted and flipped him over the side. Then dropped to the grass and stood over him with my Webley. "You can't win." I said. "Drop it!" I kicked the gun out of his hand. "I have dispatched twenty-eight of your fellows. Make your choice, the gaol or judgement by a higher authority!"

He knocked my leg out from under me. "Die, Holmes!" He lunged for his gun and took aim. I shot him, one bullet through the heart.

My search of his pockets revealed him to be Simon Worth, an Englishman. Clean fingernails, the scent of red wine, and his gun fitted his hand as if made for it. Calluses on right-hand middle finger yellowed from tobacco, and shirt British tailoring. Cracksman tool in his hatband possessed of a Dover train ticket plus a wad of the Queen's pound notes in his wallet. I didn't wait. It was clear I was in as much danger here as in London. My decision to return validated, I gifted the horse to the stable boy.

The stirrings of the Italian Irredentism in this area allowed me to slip through a confusion of magistrates. Eight hours later via rail travel south to *Genoa*, I hired a winged schooner. Powerful winds matched my resolve and swiftly propelled our sails through the Mediterranean Sea west from Italy to the French coastal town of *Montpellier*. There I disappeared into the Laboratory of the School of Medicine. During my second month I was accosted by another of Moriarty's henchmen. His present penal colony destination, the result of our meeting. At the *Gare de Montpellier Saint-Roch*, I promptly boarded the 5:22 a.m. train for my trip to the *Gare de Leon* in Paris.

I disembarked on the north bank of the river Seine, and cabbed to *Le Grand Hotel*. I inspected every face along the way, yet did not recognize my stalker. The assassin I hunted was invisible as I hoped was I. Moriarty always dressed the part, impossible to miss his black villain's cape. But cape and man were at the bottom of the Reichenbach Fall. And I was in Paris, still fighting for my life.

On arrival, I immediately cabled Mycroft. In the hotel's barber chair I was liberated from my full beard, my moustache reshaped into a Parisian's modified handlebar. Following my return to the Continent, I had completed Brother Mycroft's most recent intrigue and disappeared. Today, he was overjoyed to find me alive. I bathed and dressed in white-tie opera costume for an 8 p.m. performance of Wagner's "Tristan and Isolde" at the *Palais Garnier*. He had treated me to a box seat and the proper attire. It was a rather civilized way to return to a civilized life. I loaded and stashed my gun, handle out, in the left inner pocket of my jacket, and twirled a silver-handled walking stick up to my shoulder as I crossed *Rue Auber*.

In the opera box, I closed my eyes as the Prelude commenced from its vivid opening chord. A metaphysical hymn to love, a revelatory treatise on the nature of existence, reawakened my lost soul as the music washed over me. When the violins brought their first challenge to the oboe, I felt cold steel at the back of my skull. "There is nowhere to hide, Holmes," an English voice whispered in my ear. "Get up, drop your stick."

As I stood, I thought, Northumberland? He was hesitant to alert the audience or staff, so I had a chance. Must be a thirty-eight, from the position of the gun, he was medium height, right handed, breathing heavily, probably asthmatic. Who else was tracking me?

The box seats evacuated into the now-empty Grand Staircase. I was in front, gun at my back. As we took a descending step, I took two and pulled his legs out from under him. He let fly with a wild bullet. I lunged and knocked his gun from his hand and smashed my topper into his face. He came at me and I enshrouded him in my opera cape then propelled him down the marble stairway. He fell to the central landing. I pounced diving feet first onto him and heard ribs crack. He was now gasping for air. My gun was at the bottom of the stairs. The attacker pulled a combat dagger and hacked repeatedly at my bow arm. I flipped him and he caught hold of me, succeeding where Moriarty had failed. We rolled down the main stair, leaving a trail of my own blood. I reached for my gun, but it was too late. He had landed on his knife, and the last seconds of his brutal life bled out onto the prestigious white marble entranceway.

Shaking from loss of blood, I roared. "No, you fool—!" I shook him violently. "Who paid you?" But as life left his eyes, I knew the answer to that. Moriarty's engineer behind those perilous Alpen rock slides. My search of his clothing revealed he was an Englishman, Church's boots, with a London train ticket and pound notes in his JH monogramed silver clip. The bounty must be substantial to pull this man into it. Could he be my penultimate target? He had said "us." The amount of blood pumping out of me made immediate escape essential! I quickly discerned where to apply the tourniquet then tightly wound my scarf around my bleeding arm and left the mess for the *Sûreté*. At the hotel, I washed off the blood and sent Mycroft a telegram with my plan using the code we had devised for emergencies and caught the 6:58 a.m. train to *Calais*.

Of Moriarty's killers, I knew Britain's foulest henchman, was left, and he in turn had sent his ferocious hounds after me. This and my urgent need for medical care were reasons enough for me to board a ship pointed toward the Atlantic. I knew that to remain on the Continent in my present condition would force an unwelcome result to my lengthy crusade. Besting this man was my ultimate goal to bring Moriarty's regime to finality. "It is stupidity rather than courage to refuse to recognize danger when it is close upon you."

At times like this, it was convenient to have a brother whose fingers probed every aspect of the British government. Mycroft instructed Scotland Yard to detain the ship. On the *Calais* pier I signalled to the Aurora steamer and met Captain Mrs. Smith at the lighthouse.

"Mr. Holmes, you're a sore sight!" She said as she speedily brought her craft around and headed toward Dover. "Bleedin' all over my clean deck, that scarf won't suit." She tore my shirt into tight bandages and used them to stay the blood under my uniform.

"Promise to keep my secret, Captain?"

"Looks like they're after ya, no whiddler I. Your secret's safe wi' me, I promise."

"As is my life, thank you Madam Smith." She laughed as I doffed my cap and bowed to her.

The Aurora bore me out to the double-funnelled Atlantic steamship *Lucania*, a stalled colossus in the Strait of Dover. I was delivered with the trans-Atlantic mail. As Mate Adam Newton, dressed in the white uniform and cap of the Cunard Line, I was indistinguishable from the crew on board.

"Off wi' ye now!"

Passengers peered over the railing as Mrs. Smith blew her whistle and swiftly pulled away. The steamer had disbursed its mailbags and me onto the ship. They clearly hoped to gather an indication of why the *Lucania* had stopped, but all they saw was a new crew member who hefted the mailbags and climbed aboard. Almost at once, they heard *Lucania's* whistle.

The Captain approached me.

"Captain here is your dispatch." I said as he returned my salute.

He nodded, took the pouch, ordered the mailbags stowed in crew quarters and quickly led me beneath the bridge into his great chartroom cabin as the unimpressed passengers resumed the delectation of their journey. The first aspect of my humble plan had worked well.

Once we had reached the privacy of his cabin, the Captain addressed me. "Mr. Holmes, it is an honour to have you aboard and I am pleased to find you alive and well." We shook hands, and he continued. "I am Captain Horatio McKay, and the only other person on board ship who knows your identity. You will join the crew as a two-stripe deck officer. As such, I assign your duties. Your rank is the highest authority on your deck. It's most important that you are visible to the passengers as a seaman. Here's the layout of the ship, a list of your duties, and a passenger manifest. You will share crew quarters. Your brother said you play the violin. Do you?"

"Quite so."

"Thank you! This then is your sole duty. To perform with the orchestra, every day and evening, in uniform, as we cross to New York. The violinist we hired is seasick and refuses to come out of her cabin. Can you play her instrument, or will that be a problem?"

"Not at all."

He glanced at the blood seeping from my wounds, opened again by the climb up to the steamship's deck. "I want you to have that arm looked at by ship's surgeon, Dr. Pointon, immediately, and that's an order. Only a rare cut of beef is allowed to bleed during a dinner performance. Anything else is frowned upon." He smiled. "We operate much as a hotel does. Your new uniforms are already in your cabin, and when you send them to cleaning, they will be laundered and reappear. Questions?"

I liked McKay's efficiency, and knew he must return to the helm immediately, yet I was feeling less myself and took hold of a chair back. "The crew manifest?" I said. "Furthermore, would you furnish me with details as to who is aboard? As to the particulars of my self-defence, I carry a Webley Mark III .38 police pistol." Flipped my jacket open to show him. "And will require additional ammunition."

Unruffled, the captain said. "We can accommodate you, but please take a seat if you feel the need." I waved him off. "Chief Steward Henry Clark can fill you in on the passengers. He knows everyone. Use my authority whenever you need it. And pass along any requests from passengers to the next mate. Frank Anderson is your assistant. A cabin steward will make sure your cabin is supplied with whatever you might need, and you will find your ammunition in your room. As an officer, you have direct access to the captain—Mr. Holmes?"

Suddenly the cabin metamorphosed. Every colour but yellow had bled away and my sight washed out, legs gave way, and I saw no more.

Sometime later, sound resumed abruptly, a rhythmic pounding all around me as two voices weaved back and forth, yet what they said was unrecognizable. Time lost was impossible to gage. I lay groggy, and secured fast.

Was this one of Moriarty's old riverside lairs? Two men can be tricked into thinking they have the wrong man. I reached out with my skin's sensitivity but had no awareness, they must have used ether. Assassins went for the quick kill, but somewhere in the bowels of London, a long, slow death meant the professor's bosom friend was involved.

I could not feel my arm. There was a tight bandage across my chest. The two voices became clearer and were discussing surgical technique.

My eyes opened to a bright doctor's surgery. One I assumed to be the doctor was washing up and speaking to another. "Amputation is best introduced at the joints, wrist, elbow, and shoulder. Thank you, your help was invaluable. We needed to work fast; his arm had been bound in tourniquet too long." he said.

The assistant spoke. "Slashed to the bone! Haven't seen anything like it since my war duty, could have been bayonet wounds, eh doctor?"

I exhaled. It's Pointon.

"Something like that, I imagine, Murray. Have you read the surgical manual written by Dr. Bell, the great master surgeon of Edinburgh Hospital?

"According to Bell's technique, 'Haemorrhage is one of the chief dangers to be apprehended during this operation, especially from the axillary artery. Pressure on the artery above the clavicle is best made by the thumb of a strong assistant, who endeavours to compress it against the first rib.' Bell genuinely raises your role to an importance. You won't find this in any other treatise."

"Pointon!"

"Ah, how do you feel, Newton?"

"I don't feel anything!"

"That's to be expected." He said.

"I don't feel my arm! What have you done?"

"I used ether as an anaesthetic, more effective than cocaine."

"My arm, man, what have you done with my arm!"

"I believe I have saved it." I let out an involuntary sigh. "With Murray's help, I stitched your lacerations and then attached the bandage to your chest, so those slashes can begin to heal. No showers or swimming, stay away from the sauna and spa and any physical labour, an infection may make Dr. Bell's details necessary. Mate, you will return to me and I will re-bandage it in two days."

I took calming breaths. "Thank you, doctor. Now, release me from your bondage!" I wanted to throttle him for his consummate lack of bedside manner, but I was content to know this wasn't a torture room! Facts before theories, Holmes!

"Newton, I prescribe aspirin for your pain, and liberal amounts of brandy." He and Murray began to unbuckle my restraints. "Cocaine is not recommended at sea, wooziness does not improve one's sea legs. If necessary, come back for a dose of morphia, but you don't seem the type to sleep the voyage away. My assistant will see you to your cabin. He transported you here from the Captain's chartroom."

He helped me to sit up. "I'm Murray, a pleasure to meet you Mate Newton." He held out his left hand.

He was surprised as I recognized him like a long-lost friend and shook his hand heartily. "Murray? Surgical dresser, served in the Afghan war? Many thanks!" I thumped his back.

"How did you know?"

"Oh, overheard your conversation with Pointon."

The next morning, I convinced the doctor to bandage my arm in a way that my hand could be of use to me and after breakfast found the concertmaster, sitting alone at a table in the saloon. Lost in his gloom he was sipping a drink he didn't enjoy.

I bowed slightly. "Are you Wilhelm, the concertmaster for this ship?"

"Yes, I am."

"I am Mate Newton, and Captain McKay has assigned me to your orchestra."

He spoke to his drink. "There is no orchestra."

"I understand you need a violinist?"

Wilhelm's delight was evident as he looked up at me for the first time, left his drink and stood. "Can you play?" His voice fairly trembled.

Upon my assent, he led me to the stage, and there handed me the sick woman's instrument and sheets from the orchestra's music. As I tightened the bow, his tragic face moved through a series of expressions, with eagerness culminating in hope.

I played the appointed music, painfully and stiff, but Wilhelm didn't seem to notice. As expected, there were many Strauss pieces, yet also Bach, Handel, Tchaikovsky and even Mendelssohn, Schumann and Bruckner. "It is a spirited collection, sir."

"Oh, thank God." He exclaimed. "What is your Christian name? We are informal here."

"Adam."

"Adam, we start with dinner tonight, I'll see you here in the saloon immediately following lunch. Thank you." He thumped my back and left, while I assured him that I was as delighted as he was.

Nonetheless it was not delight I felt, but relief. I had secured an identity, a means of travel, and the security of captain and crew. I still breathed. I still lived. I had bested Moriarty. And once the brutal hunter who awaited my return was captured, Watson and I would ensure the rest would fall to Scotland Yard. I began the rhythmic rosining of the bow strings.

The reverberation of *Lucania's* engines ahead-full could be felt by all; its prodigious screw resonated throughout the ship. While I was anesthetized on Pointon's table, she had entered upon her celebrated six-day sprint across the Sea of Atlas to the harbour of New York. Mycroft will ensure my clandestine escape remains a London secret. Spies in the port of New York will be introduced to my well-seasoned artistry. Even aboard ship, I must remain ever vigilant. Surely, Murray knew of Watson and my allegiance?

Afternoon illumination slanted and shimmered through the skylight and fell on the violin. I had faced the thirty-to-one odds against me, and won each round. What's ahead will also be properly addressed. With these thoughts, I raised the violin, rubbed its wood clean with a soft cloth, and began the drills that would transform these assassin's hands into a musician's gracefully agile fingers. This I realized was the initial act of my resurrection. Performing on a borrowed instrument, poised on the deck of a steamship racing twenty-two knots across the unfathomable sea, I faced into the future and smiled.

CHAPTER 1
A NEW YORK WARNING

"...lighthouses, my boy! Beacons of the future! Capsules, with hundreds of bright little seeds in each, out of which will spring the wiser, better England of the future."–Dr. John H. Watson. "The Adventure of the Naval Treaty."

In death, Professor Moriarty had triumphed. Relentlessly hunted by his assassins, I had been reduced by their scrutiny to their equivalent. For almost three years, the august detective Sherlock Holmes had been dead and buried erased from the annals of memory. But like the "Napoleon of Crime," memory could deceive.

I landed in New York and launched my research in its Fifth Avenue Public Library. Over a dinner pipe, the *Times* gave me the looked-for details. Vassar College President Taylor was to speak that evening at the Murray Hill Hotel, Park Avenue and 40th Street, a half mile away. I arranged to be at the pub and paid the bartender for an introduction.

"That's President Taylor." The bartender nodded to him, when he arrived.

He handed Taylor his drink and gave him my card. Taylor waved me over.

I put out my hand. "Pleased to meet you, President Taylor, though still controversial, Vassar has gained quite a reputation for excellence."

"Sigerson, sit down and join me. I read your superb article recently." He shook my hand and I pulled up a chair.

"You're an elusive academic, what are you doing here?"

"Oh, recovering from an unfortunate accident. Most of my lectures and findings are of necessity at the Norwegian Science

Institute in Trondheim. My present urgency is for a quiet place to recuperate for a month or two. Might you have a recommendation?"

He listened critically, with knit brows, and quickly sized me up. His face relaxed as he came to his conclusion. "You won't achieve it in this city. The name 'Poughkeepsie' is from the Pequod Indian word Apo-keep, and signifies a safe harbour. I think Vassar College is just the sanctuary you require. What a challenge your explorations will pose to our anthropology students. What do you say, professor?"

I travelled by midnight train, at the tail end of winter 1894 and found my way to Poughkeepsie, New York. Seven days, two hours and thirty-two minutes from home. Alone in the train, the last stop, I stepped to the platform and laughed aloud. I was surrounded by a dense Hudson River fog doing its best to obscure the will-o'-the-wisp gaslight. I relaxed for a moment in its comfortable anonymity, watched the engine as it entered the roundhouse, blowing hot steam into the cold wet fog. I breathed in the smoke from my cigarette, and noted the bang and crack of river ice, mapped her distance in my mind's eye. Unseen, yet clearly marked in the shifting miasma, click on cobblestone and the clean, horsey aroma from well-cared-for animals. I stepped back straight away as the rattle of wheels, coachman's orders, and a hansom loomed out of the pea-souper. "Cab!" And disappeared into the mist, night hawks cried. The thought occurred to me, an assassin or thief could strike like an eagle and escape into thin air.

"Your cab, sir."

I turned my back to the river, pitched my bags and rushed into the apparition. "Vassar College, cabbie, Raymond Avenue, thank you." What was wholly to last six months had lengthened into years of exile. I yearned for London, Watson, and especially, Sherlock

Holmes. We travelled through the dark and sleeping town, two lit pinnacles rose on separate hilltops, the night's blackness like a sea separated them. Northward of the town a harsh, sharply lit precipice, pierced knifelike into the fog. Southward the light of a gentler summit, flickered through the mist, and it was to this my carriage was drawn.

Vassar's enormous edifice emerged like a floating Himalayan mountaintop. Mathew Vassar based the college's Main Building on Napoleon's *Palais des Tuileries* in the Romanesque style, in red brick, of all things. Nevertheless, once through the gatehouse, it was poised like an island of enlightenment. My research proved that an unusual interconnected group of five units on five-stories housed much of the college. Its central pavilion combined what one would expect to find in any of our esteemed universities: classrooms, library, art gallery, chapel, dining halls, common rooms, offices, and President Taylor's quarters. The end pavilions housed the professors, and would be my home for the next six weeks. The connecting areas housed students in four-room suites. The college was ensconced within an arboretum, filled with soon-to-blossom trees, and rolling green lawns. Out-buildings to this unique and revolutionary academy were the Observatory, Vassar Brothers Laboratory, and The Museum. The newly built Smith Building provided housing for one thousand students. Vassar's idea was catching on. It was the first in this country to offer full academic degrees to women, equal to Oxford and Yale.

I donned the bravado of my former European alias. The explorer for the Norwegian Science Institute, Professor Sigerson, was warmly welcomed by my fellows. After being shown to my apartment on the second floor end pavilion, I enjoyed a late supper of quite good shepherd's pie in the faculty parlour. Amid generous toasts to my eminent explorations, I sampled my first New York State wine.

Next morning, I awoke feeling relaxed yet out-of-place. Alone and blinking in the bright blue daylight. Instead of reaching for my gun, I reached for a cigarette and a match and took a long drag as if this were my first breath of the day. I lazily lingered in bed, finishing it. Then jumped up, put out the fag, washed, dried, and brushed. My moustache and short boxed beard had grown in well. One suit at least was ready, the rest to a local tailor today, *accoutrements* to be found in town. I ran my fingers through my long hair, such commonplace endeavours seemed miraculous after years in the wilds, and I craved them like cocaine.

I examined my wounds in the armoire mirror. Dr. Pointon's shipboard stitches had held well. I cleansed, searched for infection, and applied new plaster. Then I cleaned my gun, and loaded it, dressed in white tie requirement, and placed it in my inner pocket. My notebook I left in the drawer. On top of this I donned borrowed academic regalia. With my walking stick in my right and my left fist behind my back I walked to a first Vassar breakfast humming "The Jewel Song" from *Faust*.

A blazing beautiful Saturday, February twenty-fourth, shone through Vassar's tall windows as it warmed the air and lifted the last remnants of fog. New York City, like Paris was too formidable to keep a watchful eye. I was easy prey to anyone who knew her streets. Conversely, the remoteness of Vassar's campus was part of its inherent beauty. The Faculty Dining Room was on the ground floor. Windows on two sides looked out onto the students' village-like hallways or the pines, magnolias, willows, oaks, and slate pathways that led to the Observatory or the lab. The dark panelled wood of the walls and ceiling, tables and chairs lit by gaslight, candle, and a blazing hearth gave a warmth to my London soul.

President Taylor motioned me to his window table and poured me a cup of coffee, spoke in a low voice. "There is another reason I asked you to Vassar, Sigerson."

I was all attention.

"Your realist ethnographic approach and the fact that you are a stranger here, I feel, suits you to be an unbiased, trained observer of this vile phenomenon. Your stay as professor is not attached to this, you are free to decline."

"Taylor, please share with me all you know." I said. I closed my eyes, and put my hands in meditative pose.

"The manager of the Vassar Brewery has been threatened by an unsavoury gentleman with proposed unheard of activity in our fine Poughkeepsie. I'd like you to assess the situation and return the information to me, where with our combined experience we might find a solution. What do you say?"

"I appreciate your trust in me, and will be happy to assist you anyway I can." I said.

I returned to the Greek Scholar's table and read the headline on the front page of the *Poughkeepsie Daily Eagle*: "Poughkeepsie Ice Yacht Club Readies for National Race." My breakfast proved fruitful, from a few simple questions I gained last year's race winner and the best barber and tailor in town. An inside article proclaimed: "The Brothers Houdini! Straight from the World Columbian Exposition," performing at the Collingwood Opera House all week. I looked for London news.

Having crossed the Atlantic and awakened in another country, when my cab dropped me on Main Street I was surrounded by heralding men in long coats, top hats and bowlers and the civilized tap of walking sticks. Shouted jests from lunchtime factory companions. Subdued mirth of bustled women, their gloved hands snug in muffs. My research showed Poughkeepsie, a flourishing, middle-sized industrial city, had developed through its shipping, factories, and breweries. All nurtured by its supreme position along the Hudson.

One of the choice places for gossip, to gain a true sense of place, was the local barbershop. As I crossed Main Street, I watched the front window of Saunders Barbershop and Tonsorial Parlour filled with gaily laughing clientele. My Vassar associates had recommended the queue for Harold's chair. I entered upon a grievous discussion led by Harold which had every man involved. I suffered some of the fame of my alias as I hung my coat, and hat, and nodded to the gentlemen.

"Professor Sigerson, come right here, have a seat, a trim?" Harold brushed the hair off his chair.

"Trim the beard and moustache leave the length." Behind my hand I said. "You will need to bleach them."

Harold wrapped me in a hot towel, and swept around my feet, cleaned his tools. He gently removed the towel. And behind his hand, he said. "I'll do the whole thing no extra charge, and see you in here every week for a top up." I nodded. He slathered into my hair and beard some foul smelling stuff added it to a towel and wrapped my head in it.

He returned to his story as he lathered. "Pinto, the Italian, has done it now. He is planting a little Mafia in our Poughkeepsie town."

The other barber said, "Mafia?"

"Yes, a gambling scheme and an insurance shoddyocracy." He checked my beard.

"There's nothing illegal about either enterprise." I said.

"You're right, Sigerson. It's the way he takes his thatch-gallows debts. He gave old man Ferguson an anointing and threatened him with that knife of his." At this every gentleman's eyes turned to him.

"Did he go to the police? When did this commence?"

"Ferguson came to me to dress his wounds just two weeks ago. He was the first. He refused to go to the police." Harold removed the towel and wiped off much of his concoction.

"It is typical of such organizations to single out their victims, separate them from their right to legal protection. They become frightened of the very society that formerly brought justice in their lives. It is appalling! But effective." Harold began to trim my beard.

"The skilamalink recently approached me with his insurance deal but I treated him like the filth he is and bucked agin him strong with my broom. He's up to here on me." Harold moved his razor to indicate his chest, and shared his booming laughter with the room.

"When was this, just Pinto or others?"

"The meater slouched in here at closing, yesterday, while I was sweeping up." He pointed to his partner. "Jamison had already gone home." Harold said.

"He is watching you. Until this is resolved, it may be necessary to keep Jamison around while you close up."

"What do you say to that, Jay?" Every head turned to him.

"I'm with you! He won't have a chance. Did you know he's selling his house? I trimmed Jerry's beard this morning, he told me Pinto put out a 'For Sale' sign."

"So, this threat may be decamping shortly. What did the police say?"

"They didn't see it, said, 'Cut it, and come back when you have something." The barber said.

"The fools, did you inform them about Ferguson and how Pinto operates?"

"Yes, the goney coppers shoulda asked some of your questions. He's accosted Hyams at his department store, and Lutz at the music store. New Orleans has always had pirates. Let 'em have 'em! When Sally the Goat sailed up the Hudson, our stout Poughkeepsians sent her down with a flea in 'er ear!" Harold said. "We will keep Poughkeepsie free!" The shop patrons cheered.

"This menace seems to be generating a business owner's association. It is the way to go. Pinto will capitulate in the face of such strength. Do you own a gun, or rifle?"

"A right tumble, my Colt." He pulled it out of the drawer next to his mammoth brass register.

This man thinks, seems a natural leader. "Good, load it and keep it with you, until the threat has been terminated. Together you can bring an end to it." I said.

"Talc?" He brushed off my waistcoat.

"No, thank you, excellent work, I like the length." I handed him a silver half-dollar and my card.

"Let it grow, Sigerson, you'll look like an American in no time." He slapped my back. Oh, you may want to wash it a few times." He pantomimed his fingers like a clothespin on his nose. The shop's inhabitants laughed and the next man was seated. Harold said. "Have you gentlemen heard about the Phoenix Hose Company's 50th anniversary? Gonna be a big shindig next month."

On Main Street, I pondered what I had heard, first, Vassar, now this. Mr. Pinto is raising quick funds for some reason. Was it possible he was embarking on a business? Or had he been directed to forge this business?

I resolved to visit Vassar Brewery another day. After two rather soapy hot showers my beard was decidedly blond, and my preference for Indian Sandalwood was subtly detectable once more. There was a moment before the dinner meal and I picked up my pen:

My dear, Watson,
I composed this sketch for the sake of your notebook. I hope these few pages can recompense for my absence. I know you will forgive this rift in our time together. While completely unaware of my trials, you have remained my chivalrous Watson. Your sincere, heartfelt culmination of our adventures (precipitated by your totally erroneous conclusions at the Reichenbach Fall) endowed me with my most important weapon to outwit Moriarty's henchmen. My disappearance led me beyond the most exotic parts of the Empire, and when each domino fell, to America, the most exotic of all.

I am ever wakeful to the possibility those henchmen may still have me under surveillance. Yet they are the type to shoot first so are not difficult to flush out. My research led me to this thriving burg. Vassar President Taylor seems a fan.

I live like a scholar within this unique institution. I wear Franklin glasses and dress in the robes of my noble profession. Vassar's chemistry lab is superb. Between lectures, which are my periphrastic ramblings, and studies, you know, old man, I could I think, live this way for years, if I didn't have more prevalent issues to hand. Yet, there is a mystery here that seems to be unveiling before me.

Watson, it is my intention to compose a letter to you each morning and enfold it into my journal. After all this time, I am still unaccustomed to waking without the presence of my dear friend and colleague. Our Baker Street breakfast frequently disturbed by the arrival of a lost goose, an abandoned hat, a chemical reaction, or disturbed by gorgeous young females desperate for our help. The myriad ways our dangerous days commenced and will again, dear boy.

As you know me to be, friend Watson,
Very sincerely yours,
S. H.

CHAPTER 2
THE SCIENCE OF STRINGS

"... hand me over my violin and let us try to forget for half an hour the miserable weather and the still more miserable ways of our fellowmen."–Dr. John H. Watson. "The Adventure of the Five Orange Pips."

My dear Watson,

Six days bereft of a violin led me to a modest adventure. As you are fundamentally aware, my supercharged, highly prepared, and specialized mind requires engagement in criminal cases, chiefly murder. Music involves my mind differently and occasionally unveils the answer.

My alias is ebullient but not always welcoming, wild, vociferous, and experienced with all manner of human discourse, even if merely hand gestures and tongue clicking. Sigerson is an intelligent and shrewd negotiator, with the ability to quickly categorize and analyse the society he has chosen to study and its apparent danger. In some ways I am an anthropological detective of the species "Human." It is a good alias, and comfortable, with many parallels to my more prevalent endeavours. Yet, as you will see there are times when Sigerson fails me.

Without you at my side, more focus on my well-being is required. As you know, danger can lurk anywhere, even in an enterprising music store in this boomtown. Though you may chuckle at my venture into the land of celebrity, I rather asked for it. It is deucedly ironic that I am famous for being someone else. Although I fear if I let down my alias, the mobs would increase, as you and I are legendary in the States, through the diligence of your literary agent no doubt.

Old man, you are supremely missed. Thank your beautiful wife Mary for watching over my dearest friend.
As you know me to be, dear partner,
Very sincerely yours,
S. H.

For the delight of their clientele, Chas. H. Hickok Music Company played music on a gramophone, and today was a Strauss day. The shopkeeper showed me two violins. I had heard this man's superb talents involved both the pistol and the violin. I approached my selection as I would a case. The clues were already there in the instrument, it merely required human interaction to differentiate them. I picked up the Cremona and played drills. Then I improvised along with Strauss, as I stretched its range, checked for articulation, how fast the notes died away, its balance in a range, overall tone. "I'll try the Blanchard and your best bow?" The salesman turned off the gramophone. A small black bird smashed into the window like a gunshot. The proprietor produced the instrument, then gently picked up the starling and carried it out to his garden.

I began again. This time every test passed the scrutiny of my astute musical perception, and fingers that were sensitive enough to play a Stradivarius. It was in fine condition, a rich tone with no overt weak spots, excellent workmanship, as was the first-class black horse-hair bow. I enjoyed this violin. Eyes closed, I saturated the empty music store with a performance of the "Demon Dance" from *Faust*.

As I began, someone quietly entered the store, another came in and perched in the window, a couple arrived, another, they stood quietly. A gaggle pushed in and more filled the dance floor, or lounged on the pianos. The door was held open and a swarm flew in and joined those quietly waiting. I could hear the occasional rustle of petticoats. When I opened my eyes, the store was filled to capacity and they applauded my performance while I bowed. Then one woman fluttered forward and asked for Sigerson's autograph and I signed it. It was then they rushed to surround me, threw questions, and demanded autographs. In an instant, it changed from amusement to disputation. Repeated calling of that name became the sound of carrion crows. My jacket sleeves and hands stabbed frequently by their quills, my clothes pulled apart, ripped, pants torn, waistcoat unbuttoned, and my hat lost. One woman slashed my forehead to cut a lock of my hair. When the shop owner arrived I was smashed against an upright piano scrawling someone else's name.

True to my expectation, Herr Lutz shoved his way into the crowd. "What is this? This is no way to act! Where is your Poughkeepsie pride? What kind of welcome is this to our fair city?" He pushed a large gentleman out the door. "Get out, all of you!" He brought me back to a lounge, and treated my cuts.

"Well, well, such is fame." I said to him as I buttoned my waistcoat. "Thank you for that. When they disperse, I'd like to finish appraising the Blanchard. You are Lutz?"

"Yes. Would you like tea? It's steeped and ready."

We shook hands. "I am delighted to meet you, Lutz. Thank you, yes, no milk."

"And you, Sigerson." He poured the tea. "I put a nocturne on the gramophone, so things should calm down."

I added a sugar cube. "In Harold's barber shop yesterday I learned that you are one of the shop owners recently threated by Mr. Pinto?" Calmly stirred and tasted my tea.

He looked dubious and I quickly put him at ease. "It is laudable the way the town business owners stick together on this score." I patted him on the back. "And your handling of that unruly crowd shows how very capable you are. It is the way to success."

Lutz nodded. "Oh, he said he'd smash my violins, including the one you are interested in, if I didn't pay his insurance fee. I told him to get out of my store."

"And did he?"

"No he pushed me around a bit, but I boxed in my youth so I'm not afraid of him. Then Hyams stepped inside and he left."

"Safety in numbers is the way to advance. Did he say anything about his business or his plans?" If Lutz can handle a gun, my search for a rough and ready partner may be over.

"Only that if I didn't pay him, next time he'd bring his axe."

We exchanged cards. "Let me know of any further developments. And do you own a gun?"

"Yes. Do you really think it is so dangerous?"

"If he was dispatched here to initiate this business, the danger is considerable, and would require outside assistance." After I had refreshed myself, I asked Lutz. "Do you play?"

"A little."

"Would you mind advancing to the far end of the piano studio to demonstrate the Blanchard for me? It is one thing to auscultate an instrument playing at your chin, but quite another to trumpet it from the stage."

I savoured his presentation. "A man with such talent must share it, somewhere!"

"Here and there, there are many opportunities in Poughkeepsie. And there's a piece for two violins I have been interested in."

I began to play the "Mozart–Duo No. 2" with a smile on my face.

His eyes lit up. "How did you know?"

I laughed. "I caught a glimpse of the music in your bin, when we were having tea. We would be most suited to play it. Vassar has marvellous practice rooms. I'd like the Blanchard, the black horsehair bow with a travel case, fresh rosin, and an extra set of first-rate strings."

CHAPTER 3
ICY INDUCEMENTS

"Such a flight over the earth is among heroic feats, and it kindles your nature with the fire of valour."–Charles H. Farnham. *Scribner's Monthly*.

My dear Watson,

At this time of year, it's all about ice. Though it warmed up for a week in February, the weather recently has made up for it, ten or less degrees every day, yet clear and blue. Ice-harvesting on the river began in earnest and winter fishermen skated between fishing holes. For the city of Poughkeepsie, ice is a business, a recreation, and a sport.

Have you ever flown an ice yacht, dear boy? Poughkeepsie's frozen beach irresistibly calls a fast fleet of ice yachters. This point on the Hudson River is the centre of ice yachting in the country and the starting position for the Poughkeepsie Ice Yacht Club's yearly race. Even American "Royalty" descend from their homes in Hyde Park to fly skimmers here. But ice boating in this country has always been for the common man.

No ice yachter walks onto the Hudson without first examining Commodore Marcello's Blackboard. Its daily ice report displayed outside Meyer's Clam Tavern: "Today's report: 16+ inches of smooth black ice, perfect to Newburgh!" What the racers experience is a view of the river transformed by winter's cold into a winding, crystallized passageway, and surrounded by fir green mountains or icicled cliffs. The sails move on sharp runners and seem to fly on this ice road. When the wind picks up, the yacht soars in a burst of euphoric speed, eighty-five miles per hour. In a race like this filled with many ice yachts, expert skill is absolutely necessary as these bursts can lead to problems for the uninitiated. It's the fiercely unstable combination of speed and wind with the fragility of "paper white" sails steered more by intuition than sight that attracts adventurers to this sport. It is exhilarating! Traveling at these speeds is also quite disconcerting to would-be followers. Another fast arrow in my quiver, ole boy!

As you know me to be, Watson,
Very sincerely yours,
S. H.

Today, the Ice Yacht Club staged preliminary races to weed out the inexperienced. If the weather held, practice sessions would go on every day for three weeks. Learning to navigate an ice yacht was an intriguing addition to my skills. Because of recent out-of-doors conditioning, the boat responded easily to my directions. I pursued Shawn Reilly, the champion yachter, at Meyer's Tavern Oyster Bar. He was also the bartender and easy to get him started on this subject.

"Weight placement is key in tacking and gybing. You need to get weight on the front runner. You do this by lying down and sliding forward in the boat." He said.

I raced his boat mornings before breakfast. There were several yachters, preparing for the big day. The speed of the boat was twice as fast as the engine that steamed me here. The world became a blur in her hull. The driver and the yacht must be united reflexively, so that its operation is intuitive. A young man entered Meyer's Tavern, slapped a coin on the bar.

"Hey, Reilly, I passed the test! How's about a beer?"

He returned the coin. "It's on the house, courtesy of Vassar Brewery. Congratulations Pinto."

This man dressed like a dandy, looked a local deviant, not much brain involved, a long knife sheathed and attached to the left side of his belt, right-handed? His eyes were cruel which fit the violent man who had been portrayed to me. A singular chance had presented itself and I took my pint to his table. "May I have a word with you, Mr. Pinto?"

"What for? I don't know you."

"I've heard quite a bit about you. I am interested in your plans, and looking into Poughkeepsie's new businesses, like yours."

"Why would you do that?"

"To invest my capital in this boom town and yours is the first gambling idea I've heard. Are you interested in building a casino?"

"Yeah, with enough money behind me, right on the river, and a dance hall, too." He was clearly improvising.

"Bartender, two more pints, thank you." I paid him and opened my case. "Cigar?" He took one, I lit it and mine. "Are you married Mr. Pinto?"

"Not anymore!" He laughed and took a swig of his pint.

"A divorce in this state is a rare achievement."

"Guess again."

"I heard your home is for sale. Are you leaving Poughkeepsie?"

"Just hedging my bets. Everyone dreams of moving somewhere else, don't they?"

"Where do your dreams lead you?"

"Somewhere I can enjoy my ale in peace."

"Capital idea! I'll be in touch. Excuse me; I see it's time for my race." I stood, shook his hand, and dashed out the door.

Out on the ice, I found a remarkably strong gentleman and a young girl, commodore insignia on their sail. On the spot I proposed a race and we set off with the wind, instantly we were faster than any manmade mechanism. Surrounded by a moving kaleidoscope, my keen intuition was in control, and the bracing wind was all. I heard the sound of their blades cutting the ice cleanly.

He was good and easily twined next to my craft. But I flew the *Glacier*! With a burst of speed, I let her go, they persevered. He tacked slightly into the wind and they joined my side once again. In ten minutes we were at Newburgh, the race midpoint, I saluted and headed back to shore.

At the Poughkeepsie docks, I turned the tiller 180 degrees and splashed ice crystals in the air as I glided to a stop. They did the same. I leapt out, grabbed the rope and skated over to them. "Sir, you are an indomitable foe!" I shook his hand.

He smiled. "Yeah, aren't we? Brawn and brains united! I'm Paulo Marcello and this is my niece, Rachel." She waved.

"Keevan Sigerson. You're the Commodore! Your daily reports are most gratifying. I look forward to taking you on in the Challenge." I touched my hat and as I brought the *Glacier* into dock, my foe was being carried out of his boat. Set on the shore, he unaffectedly pulled his crutches under his arms and walked away happily chatting with the girl. "Weakness in one limb is often compensated for by exceptional strength in the others." He must have the arms of a bodybuilder and could have beaten me out there!

CHAPTER 4
AUSPICIOUS ALLIANCES

"From a drop of water. . . a logician could infer the possibility of an Atlantic or a Niagara without having seen or heard of one or the other. So all life is a great chain, the nature of which is known whenever we are shown a single link of it."– Dr. John H. Watson. "A Study in Scarlet."

My next venture outside Vassar's halls, I escorted four students to the magician's act. During our trolley ride into town, I read in the agony columns of the *Daily Eagle*: "Poughkeepsie Business Owners meeting, Saunders Barbershop and Tonsorial Parlour, Sunday evening 5:00 p.m." Capital, Harold!

We entered the theatre, and the ladies were immediately ushered to the front row. The Houdini Brothers were billed as "The Modern Monarchs of Mystery, appearing straight from their spectacular Chicago World's Fair Illusions." I found magicians foolish, yet Harry Houdini was a most singular man. His character and talent were immense! He was five feet five inches and at the beginning of his career at twenty. Yet his intensity burned up the room.

Houdini appeared wearing handsome formal wear. "Magic is the sole science not accepted by scientists, because they can't understand it. What the eyes see and the ears hear, the mind believes." He pulled a bouquet out of the air as his fiery gaze moved around the audience, and bestowed the flowers to my charges. "I am a great admirer of mystery and magic." He threw his arms out to encompass them all. "Look at this life, all mystery and magic." He pitched cards out to the audience. Each card flew through the air arcing above. The Vassar students scrambled to catch them. This was followed by his noteworthy card tricks, accompanied by the ongoing patter of his boundless positivity. It wasn't the tricks that secured the attention of the audience, it was Houdini. He was an original, his remarkable personality and the fire that burned in his eyes were what kept ours riveted.

    He and his younger brother, Dash, performed the "Metamorphosis" illusion. Houdini shamelessly drew it out, expressing the peril he would experience by staging this escape: "We may have picked up a ghost or two in Chicago. If you've been following the news, you know there are many angry spirits there. During our last performance, after being locked inside, I was sure I was not alone and when I came out, my hands were covered in blood!"

    Houdini's ghoulish showmanship carried the hour. "You'll forgive me, if I seem terrified at the thought of getting into that trunk." Dash opened the lid.

    We watched as Houdini was handcuffed, elaborately and securely tied in a sack, and then locked in the trunk by Dash. There were six padlocks, and it was also bound by heavy stout rope. Of the utmost importance was the sense of reality which surrounded this illusion. A continual knocking and shouting were heard from inside: "Get me out of here! I can't breathe! There is something in here! Help me!" Dash slowly drew a curtain across the trunk, stepped behind it, and in five seconds, and with great panache, Houdini reappeared. He threw the cuffs to the stage floor, straightened his tie, and removed the curtain. He brought my Vassar students up to the stage to undo the ropes and open the locks. Houdini lifted the lid of the trunk, and inside the sack was Dash.

    The audience rose to its feet, applauded and shouted. Houdini's *coup-de-grâce* was to invite them up to the stage to try to solve the mystery. He offered a cash prize to the one who could figure it out. Many threw out ideas, but none came close. Houdini and Dash bowed and left the stage. I examined the opened Metamorphosis trunk for a moment, donned my topper and left the theatre.

Outside the Collingwood Opera House on Market Street, I lit a cigarette. My charges were eagerly attempting to solve the dilemma, but I observed they couldn't see beyond his sleight of hand. A tall handsome, muscled young gentleman and the child from the ice boat were nearby. She was excitedly discussing the show. Her guesses proved she could regard the actual problem.

"Uncle Oscar, there has to be another way out through the back or one of the short sides, there has to be! How else?" The girl waved to our group.

The Vassar girls ran up to them. "Do you think you can solve it?"

"Possibly an auxiliary side or false bottom was used." I said, daring her to top me.

The girl looked up at me with astonishment. She blinked and it was gone. She accepted my dare and we were off. "Then when the curtain went up, Dash extracted Houdini and untied the sack."

"Then Dash is tied in the sack and Houdini pushed him into the locked trunk." I said.

"Or lowered it on top of him and Houdini donned his jacket and posed on stage." She said.

"They never had to unlock the trunk!"

"Except to let Dash out!"

The girls laughed, and Uncle Oscar shook his head. "If I didn't think they needed it more than we do, I'd say go claim your prize."

My charges surrounded her. "I'm Anne, a freshman at Vassar, what grade are you in?"

"Eleventh, nice to meet you, Anne, I'm Rachel."

"You have to come to Vassar, you belong there."

Marie introduced herself. "We have tea in the Rose Parlour at three-thirty."

Oscar Marcello and I shook hands. "I met your brother Paulo in an iceboat yesterday. He's a champion."

"My niece would agree with you." He said, as he inclined his head her way.

She put out her hand. "Professor Sigerson, I am Rachel Marcello."

I shook her hand. "*Enchantée,* child."

She looked up at me with a cat-that-ate-the-canary smile. "Your story in the National Geographic sounded hazardous."

"I find fieldwork to be refreshing and its intrinsic danger adds spice." I rounded up my students and we caught the trolley back.

CHAPTER 5
A VASSAR TEA

"Do you know, Watson," said he, "that it is one of the curses of a mind with a turn like mine that I must look at everything with reference to my own special subject. You look at these scattered houses, and you are impressed by their beauty. I look at them, and the only thought which comes to me is a feeling of their isolation and of the impunity with which crime may be committed there."–Dr. John H. Watson. "The Adventure of the Copper Beeches."

My dear Watson,

Vassar has my happy allegiance, her air is full of science and art, and the students can't get enough of it. The faculty know their work here is part of an auspicious adventure, each course stands as solid as Main. Last night we returned from Poughkeepsie and walked once again through Mr. Gatehouse's gate to enter into the comfortably cloistered and scholarly environment of Vassar. The gate is of the same design as Main and large enough for a lorry to pass through, also for a gatekeeper and his family to make their home. A most serendipitous happenstance is the gatekeeper's name is Gatehouse. And like their new library, its intrinsic humour has captured the imagination of Vassar residents who comically entitled it, "Uncle Fred's Nose." Named for the beloved gentleman who graciously made this donation, and its architectural absurdity.

With such a commencement, this trip has been enormously enhanced. The possibility of a case with all its darkness and light overshadows the genial atmosphere of this lively river town. Then again it may be a trivial matter.

Without your questions, your keen listening ability, and capable Eley's number-two revolver at my side, I will have to "Wing it" as they say.

As you know me to be, dear friend,
Very sincerely yours,
S. H.

Precisely at three-thirty the girl arrived from her trek up to Vassar. In the Rose Parlour the students' afternoon tea was underway. Marie and Anne were discussing this afternoon's lecture, which was about trifles. "But how do you know which are the important details?" Anne said.

"Am I supposed to keep it all in my head? What if I forget something important, like the tribal Queen's name? That could get me killed." Marie said.

"Every fact is important, until you decide it is not. Test them all. Practice, Marie, a principle you could be applying at this very moment."

The child had made her way through the library. She ran over and slapped me on the back. And shouted "1, 2, 3 Ring relievo!" Beneath her childish glee, I observed she was worried, hadn't slept, missed lunch, her uniform was not pressed and stuck out of her skirt, she was without her scarf and gloves. Most probably the reason for her charity clothing, I could see this was not new to her.

"Join me for tea, child?" I indicated the chair opposite mine.

She plopped into it, reached across the table, picked up my knife, slathered a piece of my bread with my butter and compote, crammed it into her mouth, then washed it down with my tea.

"My aunt is in danger! No one has seen her for days, but no one listens to me." She watched my face closely with every word she spoke. "I've read about your ability to aid others, I know if anyone can help, it is you, Professor Sigerson."

It was a cold March day, the child had walked the long blocks from her high school and a tranquil tea had been transformed into my Baker Street consulting room.

"If it is possible to discuss it quietly, child: Chocolate or vanilla? I think vanilla."

Her friends of last night brought her to the buffet, found her a teacup. She filled plates with her selections, and dropped into her chair as I was stuffing tobacco into my pipe.

She gobbled up a few sandwiches. "I know that's why you're here at the very moment I need you."

I lit my pipe. "Irrelevant, I have my own reasons for being here." I sent up plumes of smoke. "You, on the other hand, attend St. Mary's High School, are bored with your studies, are from a large family, drink red wine, are highly intelligent, need spectacles, have an amazing grip for such small hands, and hope to become a Vassar girl."

She was intent on figuring it out. "My uniform, do I squint?"

Anne and Marie brought me a fresh pot of coffee and vanilla ice cream for the child.

Marie said. "Professor Sigerson, how'd you know that?"

"Oh everyone wants to be a Vassar girl, that's cheating." Anne said.

"Ladies, use your eyes, use your eyes! You see but you do not observe." I waved them away and refreshed my coffee. Leaned back in the chair, and put a match to my pipe. "Child, this is serious. What evidence do you have?" I closed my eyes.

"My Aunt Rita is beautiful and smart. Her husband dropped off their daughters a week ago." She popped a macaroon in her mouth and continued. "It's great. We get to play a lot—but do I really squint?"

I pointed with my pipe stem. "Terminate this nonsense; you must be of an age to realize that parents sometimes take time from raising immature daughters to recuperate. I see no need for concern."

As I reached for my belletristic journals, she showed more worry with each motion. I collected my walking stick and she jumped out of her seat. "No, Professor Sigerson!"

I pointed to her chair and she sat down. "Now, I know there is a brain in there. And this tea is exciting to you, but how will you ever learn to pluck logic from the world around you, if you don't calmly give me the facts and in order!" I resumed my pipe and closed my eyes.

"A week ago the Rat, dropped off their children with Aunt Cara. Then he took Aunt Rita out, and no one knows where. Uncle Oscar saw him at a bar Friday when they were supposed to be on vacation together. So where did he take Aunt Rita? Where has she gone? Yes, we are a big family, and we see each other every day. She is the first to marry. My Aunt Rita has disappeared, and I know of all the people in the world, you can find her." Her young face flushed with determination and her eyes revealed a remarkable trust in me.

"This 'Rat,' who might he be?"

"That's what my family call my uncle, Rat or Animal. His name is banned in our home."

"The solution is simple enough. Have your family check the regulars: the local constabulary, missing persons, hospitals, clinics, and the morgue."

Her astonishment exploded as ice cream all over her dress.

"Please dear, manners, your napkin, take my handkerchief."

"The morgue—!" Her terror was quite evident. "I have tried to awaken my family."

"Then you can spend some time today securing this information?" I raised an eyebrow to her.

"Yes!"

"Straighten up in the lounge immediately." I advanced her with a wave of my hand. "Authorities look askance at such disruption."

As she left, I dispatched a few telegrams. When she came out, I said. "But are you sufficiently at liberty to fall in with me? What about your parents, your friends?"

"I'm supposed to be visiting a friend after school. I go there to enjoy the books I'm not allowed to read, like Mr. Poe and Dr. Watson. I'm expected back at six o'clock."

I nodded. "Then we do have time. Child, get your hat."

Marie and Anne joined us. "Remember, serious and logical, giggling is sure to end the interview. Call me in if disaster looms."

We four took a trolley to Market Street and the City of Poughkeepsie police station. I introduced myself and my students to the desk sergeant, and then stepped away.

Marie said. "Good Afternoon, Sergeant."

The child said. "Rita Pinto, maiden name, Marcello, of Poughkeepsie has been missing for two weeks. Do you have any information about her?"

"Sorry, to hear this, little miss. Pinto, I've heard that name, recently."

"We don't want to find—*him*!"

"Please fill out these missing person's papers."

She filled out a physical description:

"Tall, shapely, intelligent face, long dark brown almost-black hair, brown eyes, wears eyeglasses. Fashionable dress, long skirts, tight-fitting jackets, she likes stripes."

The sergeant gave a card to the child. "Professor, forget telegrams, call us next time!"

We visited each concern, resulting in the same phenomenal progression: "Mrs. Pinto *née* Marcello is not here."

We returned by four-wheeler.

At the dinner repast Marie delivered a note from the child. I opened it. Written in school grade pencil, on a torn sheet from her abecedarian notebook, I sniffed it, stained with Oxford marmalade.

"Marie, read it aloud."

Dear Professor Sigerson,

Would you be so kind as to meet me at Perry Street tomorrow after school? Aunt Marietta and Uncle Oscar would be available if you wanted to speak with them at that time. I think they're the best! And 4 of us involved in the search would be very good! Thank you for listening to me, not like that fimble-famble at the police station!

Sincerely yours,
Rachel Marcello

My dear Watson,

Well, I acted remarkably as you would have done in this situation. In profoundly missing my Boswell, I have become you.

Forget the bees, we will retire here and teach the Art of Deduction and Analysis, and the Art of twisting reality into Fiction? What do you say, ole boy?

This case could be what I require to keep me from the needle. It presents some worthy features of interest, not alone among them the Marcello family, who are far from commonplace; and the rescue of one good soul. I have always appreciated your perception concerning such damnable injustice. As a doctor, your expertise, your philosophy, tenaciously on the side of the oppressed, surpasses so many who share your vocation. Something I observed at once upon our meeting at Bart's. Have I ever told you?

As you know me to be, friend Watson,
Very sincerely yours,
S. H.

CHAPTER 6
A LADY OF RARE CHARACTER

". . . when the facts slowly evolve before your own eyes and the mystery clears gradually away as each new discovery furnishes a step which leads on to the complete truth."–Dr. John H. Watson. "The Adventure of the Engineer's Thumb."

My dear Watson,

The abundant Italian Marcello family resides in a three-story brick home on Perry Street close upon the conclusion of the Union Street hypotenuse, a comfortable residential area of Poughkeepsie. Large trees surround and fill the plentiful grounds. Soon to bloom cherry, apple, and pear form a small arbour in back near well-tended grape vines. The second and third floors are crowded with bedrooms. The basement holds casks of sweet, fermenting wine. The weight of the structure seems cushioned by its effervescent air.

Oscar's sculpture studio fills the attic. An adult Marcello is vital to my plans, he may be appropriate to the task. We will meet here. There are five brothers, five sisters, and both parents gone, died young. With the exception of Rita's predicament, they are doing well.

It is my hope that you can assemble from these basic bricks a shape that resembles your magnificent memoirs. Since this journey abroad necessitated the lack of your inestimable partnership, these humble scribblings will have to suffice. My head is lamentably crammed with words, when it should only have this conundrum before it! Watson, I will never get your limits.

I await our mutual observance of the tread on the stair, our breath quickening in anticipation, reaching for the revolver, as together we face the opening door.

As you know me to be, dear friend,

Very sincerely yours,
S. H.

Next afternoon, I cabbed to the door of her park-like Perry Street home. "This is a lovely house, are your aunt and uncle at home, child?"

"Aunt Marietta is cooking in the kitchen, making *antipasti*." She pointed to the ceiling. "And Uncle Oscar is upstairs in his attic studio, making magic. She will love to meet you, and probably stuff you with excellent spaghetti, too. But beware. Uncle Albert's wine is strong."

"You and your cohorts did exceptionally well for young ladies on your first assignment."

"Ladies, boys would have gotten lost and forgotten altogether! And none of the police or hospital nurses wanted to talk to us. They kept looking to you, instead."

I hid my smile by putting a finger on my lips. "I would speak with your Uncle Oscar about his revealing encounter with—tsk, what is your aunt's husband's name?"

"He's the 'Rat.'" She raced up while I expeditiously followed the central stair to Marcello's studio, and observed the layout of the house. At the top floor, the child was waiting. "It looks like this little lady beat you."

I moved past her to Marcello's aid. He struggled with a massive sculpture which we lifted together. He had attempted to hang it onto a pulley system.

"Yes, that's it, now we push this beam out the window, and the rest I can do. Sigerson, thank you!"

The child ran to her uncle and hugged him, getting dried plaster all over her school uniform.

I pulled out my cigarette case. "Do you usually attempt that by yourself?" I looked around the studio. "Is there anything flammable here?"

"Not today, go ahead and smoke. I usually wait for my brothers, and thank God, you saved my neck!"

I lit a cigarette and offered my case. "Your niece informed me of the World's Fair you will soon be a part of. It would be intriguing to hear what goes on backstage at such an undertaking."

I lit Oscar's cigarette. "Oh ho, politics abound through competitions and petty dramas among artists jockeying for position. Yet this is the San Francisco World's Fair, and it's worth it for the chance at such professional exposure and the friends I've made. I wouldn't miss it."

"Marcello, I imagine a man who can wrestle with sculpture twice his weight, can handle a gun?"

He looked startled. "Yes, I have a Colt .38. Why do you ask?"

"Oh, just wondering, do you box?"

"Not professionally, but I can handle myself in a fight. Strange questions, are you studying me for your next article?" He smoked.

"I am assessing your ability to be of help to me in the rescue proposed by your niece."

"*National Geographic* said Professor Sigerson is one of the greatest men of our day. And the only one who listened to me!" The child said.

"Your niece is indeed the definition of persistence. I hope you have no objection to this collaboration."

Marcello patted her head. "How did you land here?"

"I filled in for a seasick violinist on a steamship bound for New York; women are so mercurial. I enjoyed performing with the ensemble, and we disembarked in time to see the Metropolitan Opera's *Faust*, reason enough for the trip."

"Gounod's *Faust* is a favourite of mine." He threw his cigarette into the fire.

The child looked agitated but very serious. "The professor and I, and my new friends Marie and Anne, visited the police station and hospitals looking for Aunt Rita, but no one has seen her. It's twelve days, Uncle Oscar."

"Your niece has enlisted me as a facilitator in the location of your sister, Rita." The cheeriness fell from his face in an instant. The girl took his hand. "Marcello, I'd like you to relate to me exactly what happened the night you observed her husband at Meyer's Tavern."

Marcello moved to face her, and took both her hands in his. "I'm worried about her, too, Rachel. So that makes three of us. In any other family that would be enough, but this family is a three-ring circus." He looked to me. "I'd like to think she's visiting a friend in Manhattan, but I doubt it. The Rat cut her off from family and friends. Sigerson, if there's anything you can do to help Rita, the Marcello family, even if that just means me, will cover your costs."

"Thank you, I will be happy to help you with all my heart."

"Hooray, now Aunt Rita will come home!" The child said.

Marcello nodded his agreement. "Rachel, I think Marietta would like to know you're home. And she can probably use your help."

"All right I don't like it, but I love you." She quickly hugged him. "Thank you, professor." And she ran downstairs.

I waved him over. "Pray, reveal what you observed that night."

"Now that the coast is clear—" He sat on a stool and motioned for me to do so. I closed my eyes, my hands in my lap, in meditation pose.

"I was showing my friend Paul, another sculptor, around and took him to Meyer's for a drink. Always stocks ice cold beer. Best oysters in Poughkeepsie! We watched the sunset over the Hudson, colours purple, pink, and orange in a deepening blue sky with a big cadmium red sun melting—"

"Less art, Marcello, facts are what I need!"

"By sunset we were through. Luckily I saw the Rat before he saw me. He was sitting at a table on the other side with a young woman who I knew wasn't his wife. She was sitting on his lap. He was so well-seasoned I thought he'd fall off the chair. He was celebrating, and bought a round for the nearby tables, unusual for him. He got up, grabbed the table to stop his fall, took his girl by the hand and lurched out. They hailed a cab, probably to my sister's home. Good thing I didn't have my gun with me, because I could have killed him ruining my life, too."

"No, no, no." I whispered. "Do not infer; only evidence will do. What day was this, did he know you were there?"

"It was Friday. I doubt he knew anything but the girl on his lap. Paul and I waited out-of-sight for the unfolding scene."

"What is Miss Rita's husband's full name, and where does he presently live?" I pulled out a pencil and wrote his answers on my shirt cuff.

"We don't say his name in our home." He spat out: "Mario Pinto. I don't know the girl. I'm not a good source for local information. The house is on Clinton Street by the reservoir, a few lonely houses. Are you planning on seeing him? That could be fatal for you or Rita. He is good with a knife, used to batting his wife and children around. When he dropped off their daughters, they had bruises on their backs and arms. I hope to meet him in a darkened alley!"

I put my hand on his shoulder. "Something we might do together. Is Pinto a common name in Poughkeepsie?

"I know of only one."

"I am accustomed to dangerous negotiations. This type of man exists in many cultures, they do not let go easily, some will even track down a wife and kill her."

Marcello gasped.

"What is his career? And can you delineate the house, doors, and windows, is it locked?"

"Pinto drives a cab, does odd jobs." Marcello described his sister's home. "It's a blue house, grey tiled roof, chimneys on the sides. Stairs go to the front porch. Here, I'll draw it out for you." He quickly sketched the house. "There are three doors to front, back, and side. Try the back door. Clinton is deserted, houses far apart, and you can park a carriage in the backyard."

"Has Pinto shown any criminal activity, money lost to gambling or extortion, connection to criminal groups? Do you think your sister may have been kidnapped? Has your family received a ransom letter?"

Marcello sadly shook his head. "He's a petty crook, but has caused very few problems, except the terrorizing of my sister."

"He has started a protection business among the town merchants, a floating gambling concession and his house is for sale."

Marcello had a question in his eyes. I smiled. "The news I gathered sitting in Harold's barber chair. Does Pinto own a gun?"

"A gun? He's notorious for that knife he carries."

"Does he work regular hours?"

"That's a question for my sister, Marietta." He laughed. "She will enjoy meeting you."

"Thank you, Marcello. Presuming she is alive, your sister Rita will reap the benefits of the advocacy we have begun today. The officials were alerted yesterday. It may be beneficial for me to call upon you and your pistol during this search. Are you agreeable to this?"

Marcello stared at me in horror. "Of course! I pray it is not too late. And Rachel is too young for that kind of adventure. You should know that she's an orphan." We had begun our decent to the first floor and I put out my arm to stop him.

"She lost both parents at once?"

He nodded.

"How long ago did this happen?"

"She was very young when they dropped her off here and never returned."

"Was there a search? Did her parents say where they were going? What were their interests? Were they members of a church, or group of some kind? What time of year did this happen? What were their hobbies? Did they say when they would return? Did they travel and by what conveyance? How old were they and what year was this?"

"Whoa, Sigerson, I have no answers for you. We were all a lot younger, and she was a handful, inconsolable. We had just lost our father, making all of us orphans and were trying to discover how to continue on as a family. Luckily, Papa had thought ahead. When Rachel showed up we just opened our arms and welcomed her in."

"That seems to be the Marcello's way." This mystery will be docketed for now. "Your niece has advanced ahead in school has she not?"

"Yes, I am so proud of her. She skipped out of second, sixth, eighth and tenth grades."

"Was it difficult for her to do so?"

"Not at all, except for the bullies."

"Are they children, teachers, school or church related?"

"School boys, Giuseppe and I have never been able to catch them. Children are so secretive, but wounds show."

I nodded. "Your niece is an unusually spirited young girl."

We continued our walk down to the kitchen where Miss Marietta and the child were cooking dinner.

Marcello sniffed the air like a connoisseur. "Oh, my lord, this air is ambrosia; it reminds me of heavenly Venetian repasts. My goddess sister has created magic with her pots. Marietta, dear, I would like you to meet Professor Keevan Sigerson, from Vassar College."

"Oscar, I'm blushing." She playfully punched her brother.

I took her hand, bowed my head in an ingratiating way. "I am very pleased to meet you, Miss Marietta and find the Marcello family to be brimming with considerable grace and artistry."

"Welcome to our home, Professor Sigerson. I've read of your explorations in the *National Geographic*?" I nodded. "That's the way to travel, to learn and explore the culture around you. Not just lounging everywhere, giving Americans a bad name." She stirred the pot as she spoke. "Will you stay to dinner? My family is expected soon."

"Thank you, but I have a class. Even though the Persian culture differs greatly from ours, the people love their children as we do, create art, music, and cuisine as we do." Marietta nodded, and smiled in agreement. "The world's cultures are exquisitely unique, yet I find there are always places where they can connect. Even the cannibalistic pygmies off the coast of Africa cherish their children."

Marcello coughed, almost choked. "Rachel met Sigerson yesterday at Vassar and talked his ear off about Rita." He was seized by another fit of coughing. "Excuse me." He ran out to the yard.

"Do you require assistance?"

From outside we heard, "I'm okay, thanks." He coughed again.

"It's a shame he hasn't read your articles, Professor Sigerson. But Oscar's been so busy." Marietta checked her pots, stirred the tomato sauce. Bent down to open the stove, as the child handed her a large wooden paddle and she moved the pans around. The heat and heavy iron stove brought sweat to her brow. The girl handed her a towel, as attentive as a surgical nurse. The way Miss Marietta manoeuvres this enormous oven approximates Vulcan at his forge, "With a face red and fiery."

The child finished Marcello's sentence. "Aunt Marietta, yesterday we went around to hospitals and the police to ask them to be on the lookout for her."

"What?" She straightened up, wiped her forehead and neck with the towel. "Why did you go to a hospital? Are you okay? What happened? Is anyone sick? Come here and let me see!" She put a hand on the child's forehead.

She wriggled away from her aunt, ran to where I stood. "No one is sick. We filled out reports, giving them Aunt Rita's name, what she looked like, so they could find her. Professor Sigerson is helping us; he's good at it."

I was enjoying this interchange. "Of course, I will advise you of any reports that come my way. I have already spoken with your brother about Miss Rita's husband." The child picked up the wooden spoon and stirred the sauce. Miss Marietta patted her shoulder and moved away from the stove to face me as I adopted the friendly tone I reserved for ladies. "There are two points I would like clarification upon. Can you give an account of his regular work hours? Does he get along with his neighbours?"

Miss Marietta gave a quick nod, walked up to me. A whisper of Lily of the Valley in the air between us caught my imagination. "Yes, he works as a cab driver and jack-of-all-trades, and he is out of the house at eight o'clock, returns at six. I think he's working for some doctor, now. So his hours may extend into the evening." I wrote on my cuff. "Does that come out in the wash?"

"What? Oh, you mean—?" I held up the pencil and shrugged. "It must, they return unblemished."

"Who does your laundry Professor Sigerson?"

"Mrs. Hu—" I stopped abruptly.

"Your wife?"

"No—my housekeeper."

"Is she Chinese?"

This lovely woman was unmasking me in four questions. Maybe I should find out if she can handle a gun? "Miss Marcello may we get back to the point? Do you happen to know your sister's perfume?"

"Rose. Why is that important?"

"If she is there her scent will tell me. Do you have any more information about Mr. Pinto for me?"

"The Rat's dependent on his boss for hours. Rita was friendly with their neighbours." Her voice caught as she referred to her sister in the past tense. Immediately tears formed in her remarkable eyes, she turned away and used the towel to dab them. "Oh, do you think there's a chance of finding her? I couldn't bear what her life had become, but this is horrible."

The child took her hand, and comforted her aunt. I adopted a soothing tone. "Trust me, I will do my best. Thank you for your valuable assistance in this." I swept my hand to include the three of us and Marcello. "On Tuesday I invite you, your brother and your niece to meet me for afternoon tea at Vassar for further deliberations. Your niece has the details. I am most pleased to make your acquaintance, Miss Marcello." I tipped my hat. "Good night."

The child ran after me. "3:30p.m. Tuesday at Vassar's Faculty Parlour, ground floor, in the back. Good night."

"I'll be there with bells on, professor. But wait, there's something—"

I waved the child away as I cabbed up the street. Ah, Lily of the Valley, subtle, sweet, and evocative, yet, if consumed, deadly poisonous. Marietta was flirting with me in her kitchen and I wasn't averse to it. Gaslights were being lit around town, and as the warm day cooled to evening, a wisp of Hudson fog played around the horse's hooves as we ascended Main Street.

CHAPTER 7
HOUDINI'S KEY

"The importance lies in the fact that the knot is left intact, and that this knot is of a peculiar character."–Dr. John H. Watson. "The Adventure of the Cardboard Box."

Oscar jumped in front of my carriage, the cabbie suddenly reined in the horse.

"Sigerson, I'm on my way to Houdini's boarding-house. Join me!"

"How do you know him?" I said as I paid the cabbie.

"We met at the Chicago World Exposition last year." He smiled. "I was there for artistically political reasons. That's Water Street over there." We turned down the street. "His act grew exponentially, but he was non-stop. I doubt he slept or even had a place to sleep. He had nothing, but his genius. Yet he was always ready with something new for the next audience; it was a cauldron for him, and he became Houdini. I kept him fed. We ate a lot of sandwiches, drank some beer together and became friends.

"You seem considerably healthier than when last we met."

He looked at me and chuckled. "It helps to have a little acting skill when living with so many siblings!"

We ran up the side stairs, and entered into the small sitting room, where Houdini was inspecting the Metamorphosis trunk. He stopped when he saw us and shook Oscar's hand. "Marcello, can't get rid of you! Are you here to sketch me for your next sculpture? I have the pose." He reached out with both arms, stuck his tongue out, and his eyes were afire. Marcello laughed.

"That is quite reminiscent of the powerful yogic lion pose, Houdini."

"You were in the front row with all those young lovelies."

"Harry Houdini, meet Professor Keevan Sigerson."

"Oh, you're that explorer everyone's talking about, what a life, living in harems!"

The intensity and motility of his face was startling even in repose, filled with high energy, his eyes held and looked through you at the same time. A man filled with an acute sense of purpose. Strewn everywhere were unusual paraphernalia. I gestured to them with a wave of my hand, as an illusionist would do. "Houdini, what would a magician be doing with handcuffs, chains, etc?"

"Oh, just considering new ideas for my act, always looking for another angle. What would the great world explorer be doing in Poughkeepsie?"

"I teach archaeology at Vassar Female College, of course!" We laughed.

"Would you like to see what the magnificent mind of Houdini is hatching?"

Our eyes lit up and Marcello said. "You bet!" We were reduced to wide-eyed youngsters perched in our chairs.

He swore us to secrecy and then displayed his instantaneous escape from handcuffs. I deduced that he palmed the key.

"You got it! How did you do that?"

"As a magician, sleight of hand is your mainstay, and I know how handcuffs operate. It's elementary deductive reasoning."

Houdini stopped and sized me up, he shook his head slightly and smiled mischievously, "Now what do you think of this?" With the flair of a well-practiced magician, a bouquet of roses appeared in his hand.

I thought this commonplace, and then awakened to the fact that he had tied my ankles to the chair. He dared me to get out of it. It proved impossible. The knots were untameable. "Extraordinary, this is a powerful weapon and benefit to all law enforcement. Might I convince you to educate me as to their use?"

"Law enforcement! They are a closely guarded secret, sir, sorry."

I shrugged my shoulders. "That is a shame, thank you anyway. Your sleight of hand is remarkable, Houdini."

Dash ran up the stairs. "Harry I'm back! Help me carry Metamorphosis to the theatre."

I looked to Houdini. "Marcello, as I am all tied up." I turned to him. "Would you help Dash out?"

Houdini nodded to Marcello. "Help with Metamorphosis? Sure."

"And would you pick up some cigarettes on your way back, thank you?"

They carried the trunk downstairs. Houdini ran out. "Dash!"

While waiting, I reached for Houdini's copy of the *Beeton's Christmas Annual* and read from Watson's first story his list of my limits. I silenced my chuckling as I heard him come up the stairs.

"Sigerson, please, my Sherlock Holmes collection is very special to me." He seized it from me and gently placed it on the bookshelf. In one motion he slashed the knots on my ankles with a razor sharp knife. They fell tattered to the floor.

I stood and moved around, stamping life back into my feet, thanked him, then said quietly. "Your illusion has been solved, sir."

"What did you say?"

"One of the young ones after your latest show, made a spectacle of her own on Market Street, disentangling your puzzle."

"A child has done this!" He said.

"Not an ordinary child, she is probably as you were a young genius, a Mozart."

"And a girl child!" His voice rose to stage volume. "No one from Chicago 'til now, has solved it!" He pointed angrily in my face. "What's your resolution? Prove it!" Houdini incinerated me with his gaze.

I lowered to a calm whisper, and told him of the child's deductions.

"Damn! You missed a step but basically I'm ruined!"

Softly. "No, no, no, no, we can keep your secret, and haven't come forward for this reason. Please do not conclude your audience's delight, continue on as the Houdini Brothers have planned. It is our great pleasure to assist you in this way. Furthermore, you have my assurance your knots are secure with me, Houdini."

He looked at me, and shook my hand. "This is a life pact, you understand?"

"I will not reveal your secret."

"Under pain of death!" He said.

He began. "You must keep it in your head, do not write it down. This is how I do it, follow me. Yes that way, no, it goes like this, and now this, that's what makes them unbreakable, and then this to finish. You can add two of those, but in a pinch it's unnecessary."

"Ingenious, you are a scientist, Houdini. So you palm the key to the locks and handcuffs?"

"My brain is the key that sets me free. Like Sherlock Holmes I use a burglar's tool, only I hide mine in my mouth. But this is another secret never to be shared. I want competitors to think I use a key."

"Excellent and what is your rational for that straitjacket?"

"It's still a mystery." He spoke as if convincing himself. "But it has such shock value. I think the answer lies in dislocating my shoulders to get out."

I winced. "That could lay you low, Houdini, your audience is excited by the peril involved but they also want you to emerge unscathed."

"So do I!"

"Has Marcello mentioned to you that we are searching for his sister? She has been missing nearly a fortnight."

He shook his head. "If there's anything I can do to help Oscar or his sister, I will."

Dash and Marcello ran in. "Harry, it's safely there."

"Thank you, Houdini, now I'm a fan. Shall we meet at Meyer's for a pint?" As I shook his hand, he palmed me something and I surreptitiously dropped it into my pocket as I bent to pick up the tattered string. He smiled at my misdirection, and Marcello and I went down the stairs and out.

"Your cigarettes, Sigerson," he said.

I lit one. "Marcello, thank you for including me in your circle of friends, Houdini is one-of-a-kind. How is Metamorphosis?"

"Do you know they have everything laid out in sequence backstage? It's like a surgery."

"Marcello when can you meet me for some target practice?"

"Anytime."

"Tomorrow, I'll be at the river, I usually get in a sail before breakfast."

"See you then." He waved as he turned west.

In my room I found the knot Houdini had slipped me. It now rested in my violin case, until London, where it will accompany Miss Adler's photograph in my museum. To accelerate my nimbleness, I practiced tying the unbreakable beauties. A masterpiece of craftsmanship! Houdini's release from the straitjacket seemed very nearly as horrible as wearing one. I aspired never to practice this terrible knowledge.

I religiously rosined the bow strings and tightened them, raised the violin, tuned it and played the Mozart piece for two violins. I was ecstatically serene and wandering through the lyrical fantasy, enraptured by the humorous melody which pervaded throughout. The challenge of their interweaving ended in that drowsy state of sweet tranquil exhaustion which brought me to another day's rest.

CHAPTER 8
THE STORY OF MR. MORSE

"The plot thickens," he said, as I entered; "I have just had an answer to my American telegram. My view of the case is the correct one."–Dr. John H. Watson. "A Study in Scarlet."

My dear Watson,

I have been gratefully toiling in the Vassar College library, laboratory and rehearsal rooms. I know you would enjoy as I do to live here and to joust with these intelligent young ladies. That is probably surprising to you as I usually prefer the company of gentlemen. But Vassar is as revolutionary as I am and to be here at this time is illuminating. My students are alive with that desire for knowledge that has been the hallmark of my life.

My boy, even in the thick of this case, I miss your immutable aim, even when that focus is between my eyes. We are partners. Though I can work well solo for a while, for my best work, I need you at my back, filtering through my deductions, observing my process, questioning my incontrovertible proof.

Watson, I hope you are well, are happy. That this insane three-year trip of mine has not destroyed our friendship. Pray know that I couldn't live with that. But, also know that I will badger you until you give in anyway.

As you know me to be, dear boy,
Very sincerely yours,
S. H.

The ensuing day was a Sunday and the girl again associated with me at tea. After surviving a bombardment of intelligent questions about Vassar's Observatory and the science of astronomy, I led her down the pathway at the heels of Main to another of Vassar's most singular constructions.

The child and I climbed the majestic wrought iron stairway to the second floor balcony. I opened the door, and displayed the room with my hand. "Welcome to the Observatory, child."

We immediately moved into the central dome, and found the doors to the telescope open. This was unusual. My alert senses brought me instantly to a defensive stance. I pulled my gun, searched the other rooms, and held my stick ready.

Oblivious to any danger, the child was immediately drawn to the tall insect-like machine. "Isn't it beautiful, professor?"

A nondescript creature emerged out of what had looked a moment ago like a heap of old rags. I positioned myself between her and it.

Long, pale hands came up first as he cleared his throat. "Beware; meticulously fine lenses need particular handling!" An elderly gentleman emerged, with wise, intelligent eyes and a long meticulously trimmed white beard down his chest.

I relaxed, pocketed my revolver, leaned against the curved wall, and lit a cigarette.

"Put that out! Smoke on the lenses!"

I did as he commanded. He wore a straight line of medals across his chest pinned to his waistcoat.

He climbed out of his settee, and directed the child. "Put your feet there, now, that large wheel moves the whole telescope. Don't touch it! This small one on the right adjusts focus, as delicately as you would hold a fresh egg in your hand. You look through here, you see?"

"I don't see anything." She said.

"Oh you must have moved something. Let me."

She stepped down, and he moved into place at the telescope, his long responsive fingers were at home with the machine, he adjusted its height.

"But you know a view to the heavens takes acquired meditative patience. You must wait and watch as your eyes adjust to the dance of the spheres. It also helps." He cackled heartily. "To open the dome." The roof slid open, a whiff of cold air and a deep blue starry night above. "Behold God's universe."

The child climbed back up and waited with uncommon restraint for the magic to happen. "Oh, this is so exciting! I want to go, are there maps? I want to explore it all! Thank you. This is where I want to be forever, thank you, sir. There's so many, Professor Sigerson!"

"Every child has a dream; to pursue the dream is in every child's hand to make it a reality." The old man said.

I spent these moments solving the riddle of this ancient scientist. I knew he wasn't a threat. A New Englander, possibly an artist, too, who had made enough money to dress in the finest clothes (albeit twenty years old), who had travelled extensively and was connected to Vassar in some exalted way.

He turned and addressed me, "Sigerson? Not the name I was looking for. I thought you were the gentleman who almost single-handedly instructed Scotland Yard, London's populace and the world, of the proper usage of my invention, that being, frequently."

"Ha! You're Samuel Morse. But how can that be?"

"I would ask the same of you! Don't tell them, they think I'm dead, ha, ha! I have finally attained some quiet. Do you know what it's like to fight fame and fortune and battle the state and their lawyers again and again, over your own creation? 'What hath God wrought?'

"Pleased to meet you Mr. Morse, I'm Rachel Marcello." She thrust her hand out and he shook it. "And thank you."

I looked at him for a long moment, knowing he had seen through me. "I appreciate your compliment. One never fathoms the true reach of one's influence."

From the telescope, she said. "They're different colours. Can I live here?"

"My dear, you can stop by anytime I'm here, and that's only when the observatory is closed. Just knock three taps, next time."

"So, child, by following your heart's desire, you have found your way to Vassar's one-of-a-kind observatory and the esteemed scientist, Mr. Samuel Morse. So many adventures await you, here." I said.

"Professor Sigerson, my heart led me to you first." She said. I turned and found Mr. Morse staring at me.

"You are fitting in well here. Be careful, my friend, you are you wherever you are. Now, don't worry, young man, I can keep a secret."

"Yes, I appreciate that Mr. Morse. But you, sir, are one of a few individuals who have changed the world. The many lives your telegraph has saved are innumerable. It is essential to my work."

"Ah, yes, 'One's invention is another's tool.' But technology is only as good as its time, and Bell's invention is fast eclipsing mine. Good for him. It is not the inventor who benefits, but the world, as you say. And yes, there is a certain flow to technological invention, the idea doesn't come from the same source, but it is almost as if an overall design is at play and certain lightning rods attract a piece of it, until the next awakening. And you, I see, have been teaching awakening of the mind to our students."

"One monk in place of hundreds is a very different task. Sir, is it possible to aim this telescope down to earth?"

"Yes, that requires adjustment beyond Rachel's ability. Excuse me, my dear." She stood down and he demonstrated.

"Beforehand, I set up the drive, illumination system and the setting circles. Right ascension and declination depend upon your focus. The destination's ascension set, then the telescope's tube is rotated into position and locked in place, setting checked, destination checked, using slow motion controls as Rachel does, the image is fine tuned. Each wind-up covers two hours' use. Earthly imaging requires enough light to visualize your subject. What is your focus?"

"I see this necessitates an astute scientist's touch."

"Professor, I will be glad to assist your thoughts at another time. I'm sorry to say there's a night sky class due here."

"I will return when you are available, sir. Are you in need of anything, Mr. Morse?"

"I'm well cared for. I select a capable young freshman, who takes care of me. As a trustee of the college, Vassar tolerates my secret life. They say my ghost haunts it, ha, ha. When my fledgling graduates, I have the joy of finding a new wide-eyed young scientist to mentor. When will you come to Vassar, Miss Rachel?"

"Next year, but I'll be back here as soon as I can."

"Good night, Mr. Morse." We left the Observatory for a Raymond Avenue cab to Perry Street.

My dear Watson,

The child is adequately cared for by the Marcello family, yet what her splendid mind requires is not acknowledged, probably not even understood. Her aunts are intelligent, yet can't see beyond marriage as a calling. She possesses a mind that can reach the stars. Possibly Vassar is the better answer.

This estrangement wears thin. Living under an alias has lost its charm. I wanted to heartily embrace Morse's surmises, to have at least one person know me, yet, my desire for recognition would endanger his very life. Humility is not anonymity and three years wearing a spiritless name and persona is enough to increase anyone's cocaine usage.

Tomorrow's task could be nothing, or could prove considerable. Though some of my skills have been honed and even surpassed a sharpness not seen since youth. In this case, as in all, facts are what I need.

Raising my violin I improvised through one of your favourite Mendelssohn Lieders and imagined your face softening to the music. Soaring on the fantasy, I swoop in and around my muse as she playfully counters every parry and found my next moves fully formed, the image appearing like a photograph developed in fresh chlorohydroquinone. I laid down the Blanchard and began my work. Watson, you illuminate me!

As you know me to be, dear friend,
Very sincerely yours,
S. H.

CHAPTER 9
THE RAT

"He is one of the most dangerous men . . . a ruined gambler, an absolutely desperate villain; a man without heart or conscience."–Dr John H. Watson. "The Beryl Coronet."

My dear Watson,
I have my tools in hand, my revolver pocketed. Strange to be doing this without your watchful eye and steady hand, but it points the way to an expeditious unravelling of the central mystery. You know, old friend, in this my conscience is unconcerned. If I wind up incarcerated in a Poughkeepsie, New York, stockade, please be easy with me.
As you know me to be, dear friend,
Very sincerely yours,
S. H.

At 9 a.m. I became a Hudson River Telephone Company installer. I had made significant changes to my face with subtle makeup, nothing that would compromise me in a fight. The plan was to approach through Pinto's backyard and search for evidence of Rita's whereabouts. If discovered, would let my fists speak for me.

The house offered little resistance to a master cracksman. My tools worked as easily as a key. I silently entered and began my systematic search. The house was quiet, entrances locked, front, back, and side. Windows in front, lumber room to the left of kitchen and the sitting room ahead, fireplaces cold, gas off. Bedrooms on the second floor, dressers showed two weeks of dust on once-polished surfaces. Search of the closet showed flowery and feathered dresses, dove-grey silk with ostrich feather trim. He had moved to his next victim. On bed pillows I found a few strands of blond hair. On the dressing table, her powder, her perfume, hyacinth. Not rose. Bed unmade with men's clothes thrown on it and the chair. The children's bedroom yielded little, yet I had found treasures to return to each of Rita's girls.

In the study, next to the bedroom, a desk covered with a large pile of unopened bills. I probed further. A false partition opened, and squirreled deeply within, I found a legal document and sequestered it immediately in my inner pocket.

On the ground floor, I inspected the sitting room fireplace, and found small unburnt scraps of striped material. I heard him before I saw him. Pinto stalked in with a double-sided axe in one hand and a throwing knife in the other. My whole attention was with the axe and the window I knew was at my right. He started for a moment as he realized his investor had paid him an unwelcome visit. Enough time for me to move to the window then step back as he threw his knife and shattered the glass, I leapt out, and instantly the axe followed. I scaled the porch roof, and groaned as if hit. When Pinto came out looking for me, I pounced.

He smelled of stout yet not of horse and snarled like a rabid dog. Thankfully his hands were now empty. "Bastard, devil, thief, what's your game, Mr. Investor?" He jeered as he gained his feet and swung a right, aiming for my chin.

I sidestepped it, moved closer and threw a straight left, which hit him square on the jaw.

Pinto threw a big roundhouse punch, which I easily ducked. He threw another. I ducked it, then stepped in with a low left to the body. He threw a right-handed punch, which I blocked. Then I hit him with another left. He came at me like a madman, and threw a wild jab.

I grabbed his jabbing arm, and turned it behind him, then pushed him with my foot. Pinto the bull roared and ran at me, again.

I hit him cleanly with a direct cross-hit under the jaw and he spun round with the force of it. Pinto fell to the ground. I added a hard, disorienting slap to his ear which allowed me the distraction I needed to secure him.

His ear was bleeding and he screamed. "I'll see you in jail, filthy thief!"

"Where is Rita?"

"What the blazes, I annulled that crazy witch."

I held up the rope he was tied with, cleared my throat.

Pinto yelled. "Nothing you can do about it, the hospital says it's final. Let me go, untie me!" He rolled over to knock me down. I stepped past him.

I pointed my gun to his good ear and cocked it, then disappeared before he realized I'd gone. He shouted out as I calmed the horse, leapt to the cab, turned onto Clinton Street, and then expeditiously brought the horse to a gallop. His profane litany proved Houdini's knots were holding.

"You dirty, thieving villainous bastard! I'll Jesse you! I have a lot of fists in this town! Untie me, you boat-licking swine! I'll rumple your feathers, give you a good anointing. You damn son of a bitch! I'll show you. Thief, robbery! Somebody help me!"

I tore off the uniform in the Vassar Brothers Laboratory. In my vest and trousers I wiped off the majority of my disguise, wishing I could as easily remove the putrid taste from my mouth. I burned it in the furnace, washed off the rest of my costume and donned my robes. Then walked to my apartment in Main, where I examined my arm. I donned grey tails and topper, and was pleased to welcome myself again.

I happily recognized the return of my restraint, for I did not kill him. To celebrate, I went out with a Tchaikovsky waltz on my lips, and drove my cab down Mill Street to Schoonmaker Stables. At the river, I joined Reilly at the bar to share our common enthusiasm for ice sport over an oyster and cold ale lunch at Meyer's.

CHAPTER 10
A CHAIN OF EVENTS

"There is no great mystery in this matter," he said, taking the cup of tea which I had poured out for him; "the facts appear to admit of only one explanation."–Dr. John H. Watson. "The Sign of Four."

My dear Watson,

Yesterday, I deliciously disposed of another slogging ruffian, still got it, ole boy. The case is indeed looking up. I now know without a doubt that my quarry is alive and safe for the present. It is remarkably excellent news for my clients. All it took was a little breaking and entering, useful in a good cause, eh, Watson?

Now I present the facts I have gained to others. They will welcome some, be distraught by the rest. But without you, dear Boswell, I am lost again, your beneficent responses fill in much. It is impossible for me to tell the story in the same way, which leaves my summing-up decidedly flat.

I was pleased to note that Vassar serves as close to a real English tea as is possible here. I tutored the staff in how to steep tea correctly in china, and maneuvered fresh cream, cubed sugar, and bees' honey into the mix. For today's visitors I brought in sandwiches with assorted Italian meats and cheeses.

Ensconced in a corner of the Faculty Parlour, I scanned the newspapers in that disinterested way you have described to our readers. I had pre-arranged four chairs around the table and placed Marietta next to me, to better gain her trust.

As you know me to be, friend Watson,
Very sincerely yours,
S. H.

When Miss Marietta, Marcello, and the girl arrived, they found me wearing grey tweed and Irene Adler's token attached to my watch chain. As they approached, I stood, seized the newspapers from the table, and threw them to the floor, then reached my arms out to them. "Welcome to Vassar!"

Marcello comfortable in his sculptor's wool hung up his coat, then the child's warm blue jacket and cloth cap. He greeted me. "Nice place Vassar. But where is their statuary? I can see the one I'm working on right now standing proudly in front of the Museum."

Marietta was enchanting in dove and pink velveteen, with a smart fitted wool jacket and long skirt. I took her hand, led her to the closest chair, and noted her delicate perfume. It was becoming difficult to ignore, yet I wasn't a novice at this. "I'm very happy to see you again, Miss Marcello."

"And you, professor."

I shook Marcello's hand. "You might talk with President Taylor about that. He would be interested in a local, classically trained artist. Have a seat and please help yourself to my cigarette case. Yesterday was a vigorous and successful day. The situation is indeed looking up."

Marcello lit a cigarette.

"Do you take milk with your tea?" Miss Marcello nodded. I poured, sat down, and lounged in my chair. Then spread my hands out to include the inhabitants of the table. "This hopeful conglomeration is here for one purpose, to help Miss Rita. There is a strong possibility of successfully achieving this task." I sipped my coffee, lit a cigarette.

"Let's do it!" The child said.

Marcello spoke, with some embarrassment. "Sigerson, I don't know how to say this, but my family has given up on Rita. Her husband is ruthless and fought with everyone. My brothers faced him down, and he moved her away from us. Now he's spirited her away someplace."

"Is there no way out of a cruel and dangerous marriage for one such as Miss Rita?" I said. "The Almighty has given such grace to the flowers, is there none left for the exquisite flora that is our contemplative mind? How could your sister be abandoned to spend her life thus? With your help, we have a chance to find her. But we must act." I put out my cigarette, refreshed my coffee.

Marcello put his arm around Miss Marietta. "Marietta and I are ready to act on Rita's behalf. Nothing would stop us from bringing her home."

"What is your news, professor?" The girl said.

I lit a cigarette, sat up through my plume of smoke. "When I interviewed you, I was looking for possibilities, specifically ways to locate your sister." All three were fixed on me and holding their breaths. "From your answers I realized that my only forward routes were to face Pinto or search their home. With the precise information you afforded me, I walked effortlessly in through the back door.

"A fortnight's worth of dust and unopened bills greeted me. A house not cleaned, showing signs of male-only habitation. A closet full of flowery clothing, scraps of striped material in the fire ashes, signified he had moved on." I passed an envelope to them. "All showed the dearth of Miss Rita."

"I searched the bedroom, and then the sitting room before Pinto attacked me. I am a practitioner of the eastern martial art of Baritsu, which has come in handy before. I simply disabled and secured him. Behind a false desk drawer, I had already discovered a legal document." I produced a folded paper from my jacket pocket and read: "Section 1146-A Of The Civil Practice Act Of An Action For Annulment Of A Marriage." I handed it to Miss Marietta, who took a breath, studied it and handed it to Marcello.

"You're a wizard. But why was he home at all? Are you all right? He didn't hurt you?" The child said.

"A first-rate question, in my travels, I have had to prove myself many times. Mr. Pinto was subdued in a matter of seconds. Yet he did tell me what I wanted to know. Your sister is in the Hudson River State Hospital in Poughkeepsie." Their faces fell. "Yesterday, I corroborated Pinto's ravings via telegram." I opened it and placed it on the table. "She has been there for the last two weeks." I struck a match and lit a new cigarette.

Marcello gasped in horror and picked up the telegram gingerly, as if it were a venomous snake. "My sister Rita in an insane asylum!"

Quietly. "Thank God, professor, I think the heavens guided you to us." Marietta said, clasping her hands together. "Oscar, she is alive and well."

"Let's go get her, please!" The child jumped up. She pulled on her aunt and uncle's sleeves.

"Rachel, sit down! Forgive me, I also wish we could take Rita out, but it's not that easy. There are legal matters we must face first. We don't want to make things worse for her." Then Miss Marietta's face brightened and she looked to Marcello and me. "The animal has annulled their marriage? He's finally done something right. This means she is free of his control, and if I'm correct, we can now act legally on her behalf."

I re-evaluated her. "Exactly, Miss Marcello, yet, we don't know what condition she is in right now. She may be confused, drifting, and recuperating from his abuse physically or emotionally. While in that dark maze, she can only succumb. An intelligent woman like your sister would understand that. So yes, she is safe, for now. Our next move is to find a private doctor to assume with your family the responsibility of caring for her independently. This physician will give us more information about how to authorize her release. That is Monday's adventure, and this will be a tough assignment are you up to it, child?"

"I'll be there." Rachel said.

"Be careful, Sigerson, if this is dangerous, it's not appropriate for Rachel!" Marcello said. I waved him away.

"But we can visit her?" said Miss Marietta.

I nodded. "Admirable idea, Miss Marcello, you may also alert your sister to our scenario. There will be a court date, and a proof-of-sanity examination. I would advise you to bring her a suit for both of these events. All should transpire rapidly, in the next weeks. The family will require a lawyer to represent them. Do you have one?"

Miss Marietta and Marcello conferred with each other and she shook her head. "No."

"Then a lawyer for your sister's liberation will also be produced. I'm curious, why did Rita involve herself with Pinto?"

"He was handsome, dashing, and dangerous."

"Danger is an attractant to ladies? Surely, the opposite is true."

"No it is exciting!" She said with a twinkle in her eye. "He was a lot of fun at first, had an ice-boat and taught her how to sail it, used to sneak her into places ladies are not supposed to go, was impulsive, and he didn't play by the rules. Rita has always been outspoken, outgoing and desperately wanted to leave home. A tight-knit Italian family was stifling to her. To live with an overbearing father is one thing, but five overbearing brothers, is something else again. Forgive me, Oscar. At the start, he was protective and appreciative, and he had his own house. You know how blind love can be, Professor Sigerson?"

"I have observed people make the worst decisions in the thrall of it."

She searched my face for a moment. "Rita didn't see any warning signs. She watched him win a knife fight and he generously bought the loser a drink, no hard feelings. It all seemed planned to me. He changed dramatically after their children were born, horrible man!"

Miss Marietta took a deep breath, looked up and her face brightened as she punched Marcello and smiled. "Why don't we have a birthday party at the asylum to pass along information? Maybe there's time to run over there now? It's barely sunset, and we can let them know we will be there in two days. And leave a note for Rita, too. What do you say, Rachel?"

"Yes, thank you!" She looked gratified, yet sobered as she turned to her aunt. "Aunt Marietta, I want to come along on that birthday visit, too." Miss Marietta patted her hand.

"There is another conclusion of which to apprise your family and the answer to your niece's question. I amply adjudged Mr. Pinto's status from his condition, his attire, the time of day, the alcohol on his breath all pointed to a recent loss of employment. Men under such circumstances can become desperate."

Miss Marietta said. "You've thought of everything, professor. I am grateful for your work on our behalf. You faced down that animal, putting yourself in danger for our family. It's clear you genuinely can help us, yet how will our family accept this? To care for our sister who has been in an asylum? We are not nurses. We don't know how to do that." She paused and then resumed in a sadder tone. "Oh, poor Rita. Oscar, you know there will be much more said when we bring this home."

"Aunt Marietta, the whole family looks up to you and Uncle Oscar. You can convince them and then Aunt Rita can come home."

Miss Marietta said. "Child, you don't understand the world of adults and what our considerations are. I wouldn't know where to begin. What if she hurts herself, or someone else? No, this has to be thought out. I realize you have not done so."

"Marietta, you raise important issues. What are those considerations? The smallest chance of giving Rita a better life is worth any risk, isn't it? If I were in that snake pit, I'd want your help." Marcello put his arm around her and hugged. "Rachel's right, if we talk with a few and get them gossiping, and lead the discussion at dinner tomorrow, we will see."

With a sweep of my hand, I indicated our association. "Together, there is such hope for success in this ingenious collaboration." I stood, and dressed in my robes, like a jacket. "Please excuse me, I have a class. Child, you are welcome to join us. Enjoy the tea, Miss Marietta. I would accompany your birthday party, if I may?" She smiled.

"Sigerson, I worry for your safety after humiliating the Rat like that. You don't know him." Marcello said.

"We'll meet at Meyer's 5 p.m.? Vassar just doesn't have the oysters. And you can tell me all about it." I left.

At 4:45 p.m., I patted my pistol in my jacket pocket, and cabbed into town for dinner. One after another, the gaslights dimmed in each store and doors locked for the night. The street darkened by a succession of sequential increments. I descended the cab at Main and Washington Streets for the Post Office. Then continued my walk down Main Street with Perry Street ahead of me and beyond to Meyer's. What happened next would fill the pages of a yellow-backed penny-dreadful.

CHAPTER 11
THE MEN FROM POUGHKEEPSIE

"Mr. Sherlock Holmes!" roared the prize-fighter. "God's truth! How could I have mistook you? If instead o' standin' there so quiet you had just stepped up and given me that cross-hit of yours under the jaw, I'd ha' known you without a question."–Dr. John H. Watson. "The Sign of Four."

On this cold March night, Main Street's gaslights were as yet unlit and the river fog rising. Was it the plummeting temperature or an abrupt sense of danger that prickled my skin? I wound my scarf around another time and turned my back to Washington Street, intending to continue west to Meyer's in time to meet Marcello. At Perry Street, I stopped and packed my pipe with the local tobacco and cupped my hand over the bowl to light it in the shelter of the Pottery and Drain Pipe Factory. A red-faced giant of a man grabbed me from behind and held fast. I struck him with my stick but the grip of his enormous hands was like iron. His vice-like arms smashed my pistol into my ribs. Out of the factory's shadow Pinto strode and knocked my stick away. I struggled for a defensive position but it was impossible. There was only one way in or out, my kicks landed yet were met with indifference.

Not an assassin! I began to laugh, loud, hearty and uncontrollable, as I was dragged back into the gloom.

"Stop laughing, you clown! Think I'm dumb? Think I don't have friends? What are you investing in now?" Pinto's punches aimed at my chest and abdomen, above and below the behemoth's iron bands. He peppered each one with a curse. "Damn! Devil! Bitch! Break into my house? This is how we treat thieves in this town!"

All I could do was proclaim my presence and hope someone heard me.

Pinto pulled out his long-handled knife and slashed through my shirt, not deep enough to hurt me, yet it was first blood.

I acted my part and bellowed!

With a degree of satisfaction in his voice, "You can't trick me and get away with it! Watch his feet, Tito!"

I heard shouts and someone running toward us. I groaned loudly. I had sagged feigning hurt, and now was able to land a solid kick at Pinto's knee as he came at me again. He yelled. "*Bastardo!* I was going to let you live, but now I'll let you die."

Racing from Perry Street Marcello crossed Main Street to the factory. He sounded like a hero from the pocket novels Watson enjoyed and pointed his gun at Pinto's temple. "Let him go!" He demanded, and then laughed in a vile way in a tone I had never heard from him. "I have always wanted to meet you in a dark alley with a gun in my hand and here I am, living my dream. Let him go!" He laughed again harshly. "You're going to jail for this. How drunk are you? Fool!"

Then from Main Street, whooping it up, shooting their guns in the air appeared the barbers, Harold and Jamison. Tito dropped me. They sat him down. I gained my feet, and nodded to my rescuers, pointed at Pinto to join his associate on the ground. Professionally searched my attackers, collected their knives and billy clubs, and gave them to Harold. I whispered to Marcello to hold them while I rushed the few blocks to the Grand Hotel and alerted the police. "I will not return, don't give me away."

Pinto attempted to persuade Marcello. "Oscar, this is nothing to you. You get involved and you'll be next."

Marcello cocked his gun. "Fool, this is a hair trigger. Save it for your confession!" On Market Street, I took a cab to Vassar.

Later, Marcello informed me that the police brought them to the station, Detective MacKinnon took their statements, and let him and the two barbers go. They congratulated themselves on the adventure and Marcello cabbed to Vassar.

He knocked on my door and dashed in, just as I was putting the needle away. I laughed. "Marcello, with that gun in your hand you sounded like someone out of a dime western. Save it for your confession?" We laughed.

"Please hang up your coat and take a seat. I require some doctoring after being so painfully threatened."

I had dropped my coat and jacket, collar and tie on the floor, festooned the college statuary with my hat, and had already assessed there was no damage to my arm.

"Marcello how can I thank you? You may have saved my life."

I peeled off my bloody shirt, washed up and applied an antiseptic. Secured both of us a brandy, but remained shirtless, for my ministrations to dry.

"The bleeding stopped. You're right; he is good with a knife, a light touch to start the flow of blood, a scare tactic." I laughed, sipping my drink.

"What happened to your arm? Are you okay? He was hitting you hard."

"The gentleman who knifed me during my recent expedition is presently standing before his God, and the result of this scuffle is nothing rest will not cure, thanks to your most welcome involvement. The first rule in boxing is to learn to take punches, Marcello."

"You killed him?"

"He attempted to kill me. During our skirmish, he fell on the combat knife he had used on my bow arm."

"Why did you leave?"

"I ducked out of the limelight, Marcello. A run-in with the constabulary would spotlight my whereabouts."

"Are you hiding from the law?"

"No! I am in concealment from lawbreakers." I held up my arm. "And I am regenerating from my last encounter."

"Sometimes I forget your life is not an ordinary one. What are those marks on your left arm?"

I laughed. "Marcello, you are not so innocent as that? I occasionally use a 7% solution of cocaine."

"Why would you? Isn't that ruinous to your health?"

I lit a cigarette, offered one to Marcello. "The solution I use is safer than most. But a gentleman's single vice is unimportant."

"I told the police you had run away and we never got a good look at you."

"Quick thinking, thank you, your bluffs were superb."

"They weren't bluffs for Mario."

I laughed unreservedly. "Harold and Jamison running and shooting their drawn pistols in the air like cowboys!" I shook my head and howled.

"How are you feeling? If you are up for it, Sigerson, would you play your violin, from one artist to another?"

I picked up the Blanchard. Gounod's *Faust* naturally built from the early low notes. Each was given its due, and then took off as my high notes flew across the Hudson.

Marcello sat spellbound and took out his sketchbook.

Eyes closed, my new violin expressed all the voices of the opera. I performed the demon's dance with ferocity: Faust's yearning, Mephistopheles' lies, and Margarete's beauty were painted accurately. The martinet soldiers and an archangel's intervention were all awakened through my bow. The music danced with the ancient spirit of the Hudson River. Acknowledging the river's virtuosity, my strings sang with its strong, clear winds, splashed in its deep waters filled with life and the wild beauty that defined all who lived near her majestic shores.

I opened my eyes and Marcello handed me my glass. He toasted my performance: "Bravo, Sigerson, you moved me far beyond myself."

"Thank you I am not favoured much with the company of artists. Yet, for me, music is the most sublime way to involve the mind."

"I wish Rachel could find that."

"Marcello, I understand your niece's intelligence and its associated problems. It is lonely to be in a world where you are the only one who can think this way. As an artist you understand?"

"Yes I do."

"I would like to recommend that she skip her twelfth year and start at Vassar in the fall. It is the singular institution for her. She will thrive there."

"Vassar? How can we swing that?"

"I have started a scholarship for her. And I feel sure President Taylor will grant her another. He met her informally at tea. But please keep this to yourself. Since I am leaving in three weeks, I would rather she looked forward to her career at Vassar, than focusing on my part in it."

"A wonderful gift, Sigerson, thank you. You're sure she wants this?" I nodded. "Then I'll see what I can do. If Rita were here she'd back you up one-hundred percent. But, please join me in Manhattan, Sigerson. We will pack our freight car for the Fair, and you can view some of it."

"Thank you, I would enjoy that. In return, I invite you to consider a London trip. You will be most welcome and I would enjoy showing Miss Marietta the sights. Has she travelled?"

"Do you mean that? My sister is not a piece of wood, she has feelings, I've watched you flatter her when it fits your plans and just drop it."

"And—? Marcello, it is imperative that I return to London. Do I act on tender feelings and then abandon her?"

"She could go with you."

"Do you think she would? I don't see it."

"You could give her the chance to make her own decisions."

"Hmm, good point, but, Marcello, freeing Miss Rita, is our focus and we barely have time for that."

"Yes, you're right." He looked at his watch. "It's late." He threw down his drink. "Thank you for your top-notch *Faust*, goodnight and take care of yourself."

We shook hands as he walked out the door. "I am lucky to call you friend."

I then sent a telegram to Harold:

"BRING YOUR GROUP'S EVIDENCE TO DETECTIVE MACKINNON. AND THANK YOU BOTH FOR YOUR RIP-ROARING RESCUE. S."

My dear Watson,

Oscar Marcello is a remarkable young man and a talented artist. I hope to introduce him to you. I have made two, possibly three good friends and one enemy here in New York.

Americans have such directness, such an ease of being with one another. What they lack in social graces is made up by their openness and freedom of speech.

Marcello saved my life tonight, as you have done on so many occasions, my dear fellow. When I was toiling in the wastelands, one thought warmed me, knowing that if you could, you would be by my side facing death along with me, my dear partner.

As you know me to be, old man,
Very sincerely yours,
S. H.

CHAPTER 12
A DAWNING LIGHT

"Here I was trapped into an asylum, consigned to a living tomb, as completely shut away from the world as if I had never existed. No one knew where I was, no one would believe a word I said, I was numbered among the insane, although in the same condition as I had been in all my life!"–Clarissa Caldwell Lathrop. "A Secret Institution."

My dear Watson,

When you approach the frontispiece of the Marcello home, there is an enormous old sentry oak which welcomes one into a grove of sheltering trees. Alike to many in this town, the house is red bricked with ample fireplaces and brimming with the life within. From the front door there is a large, sunny portico filled with comfortable rattan. A hallway with family photographs on the walls leads to the sitting room. A wide stairway advances to the second, third and the attic floors. Marcello's studio is up top, yet his sculpture adorns every wall, table and mantelpiece.

On the right is a dining room fit for a manor house, an enormous patriarch of an oak table, chairs, and cupboards. The kitchen is to the left. Its door opens out to a grand lawn, with large, overhanging pergolas for frequent parties on the flagstone patio.

Dinner is a happy, yet raucous affair at the Marcello house. If you prefer serenity with your meals this is not the spot. Not Mycroft's taste, but I suspect it would be just your cup of tea, old boy. The Italian wine tradition is observed. Everyone, no matter the age, is expected to share the spirits.

My hope, old chap, is that I will be with you again in three weeks' time to restart our mutual adventures, especially the one that waits unfinished.

As you know me to be, dear friend,
Very sincerely yours,
S. H.

This singular family council was reported to me by Oscar Marcello after the fact:

Miss Marietta and Marcello took the lead in this most unique family gathering. They had begun at breakfast with hints and speculations to pique the interest and presently the after-dinner conversation would commence with some unusually weighty discourse.

Altogether, there were ten Marcello siblings and three nieces. The child was present. Miss Rita's two young daughters, Alessa and Silve, were upstairs asleep. And of course Rita, the subject matter of tonight's discussion, was absent.

Felice strummed his guitar in the background. Albert refilled glasses with his homemade wine. Miss Marietta quieted the din, tapping her glass with a spoon. "I'd like to start the discussion of Rita's dilemma and what we will do about it. The situation is that Rachel has hired Vassar Professor Sigerson, the explorer, to find her. And he has." Her family cheered this bit of information. "He found her where the Rat abandoned her, in an asylum." Her sisters gasped. Italian curses escaped her brothers' usual reserve.

"To bring her home, we need to hire a lawyer and a doctor for the court sanity hearing, which is in ten days, and I would like us all to be there. Following that, the professor, Oscar, and I will take her out of that horrible place."

"Look, as far as I'm concerned, I want Rita out of there and home. Never felt good about that *Cretino*." Felice said.

Albert complained that she chose the Rat and turned down his good friend who would have given her a good life, so now she had to live with her own problems. "No, I don't care what you say. Nothing will convince me to bring that woman back here!"

Camila said. "Albert, enough about your friend! Oscar, how will we support ourselves and pay for her lawyer and doctor, too? We are not swimming in gold. We have expenses, food, gas, taxes, church, clothing and shoes for three growing children."

Dona said. "How do we know this doctor will help her to get better?"

Giuseppe jumped in quickly, before the others. "Think of what you are asking. If she's locked up in that place, no one thinks about her."

"Listen to him! If we bring a crazy woman here, everyone will think we're *allocco* too!" Albert said.

"And how will we find wives and husbands? We will be outcasts in Poughkeepsie. Has anyone thought of that?" Giuseppe said.

"Uncle Giuseppe, your sweet Elena will still marry you." The child said.

Camila put her hands on her waist. "Hudson River State Hospital is brand new. Marietta, don't you think Rita's where she belongs? I heard it's modern."

"Don't we do enough already?" Giuseppe pointed to the children's upstairs bedrooms. "How could we help her, anyway?"

"Women are crazy, especially her; it's in her nature, she belongs there." declared Albert.

Cara stood up and put her hands over the child's ears. "Albert, don't let Rachel hear you say such things. You'll make her one of those suffragists for sure. And I just might join her. I think Rita could be more of a help than a hindrance around here. And there's no reason she couldn't get a job, after a while."

"Lunatics are violent." Albert said. "She could hurt Rachel or one of us!" He pointed upstairs again. "Those kids came here all bruised, open your eyes!"

Oscar said. "My sister is not crazy! Remember who put her there. He's violent and ruthless. It's another way the Rat found to be cruel to Rita and her children. Come to the asylum tomorrow if you want to be reminded of how strong Rita is still."

Disturbed by his thoughts, Giuseppe spoke up. "The church will excommunicate us all if she comes back home, their marriage was annulled! She can throw away her soul, but I won't go to hell for her problems!"

"Annulment doesn't lead to excommunication, so you can relax, Giuseppe. Marietta pointed out only yesterday that this annulment is good for us because now we can legally act on Rita's behalf." Oscar said.

"Oscar, these are serious questions. A lot is at stake!" Giuseppe pounded the table.

"Who's going to pay for this lawyer? Are you?" Albert demanded.

Marietta said. "Many of my sisters and brothers do not listen; the mystery of our lost sister is solved. Oscar and I will next find a doctor and a lawyer for the court. Giuseppe, you mentioned hell that's where Rita is right now, not a hospital. The screams Rachel and I heard coming from that hellish nightmare last night! I want her out as soon as possible and we can afford it. Would you want to hear we bickered over money if you were locked away too? I doubt it. There are loads of unhappy people in that place with no chance of rescue. We can show what a loving family we are and save Rita from the suffering those people were screaming about.

"I went there yesterday to reconnect with Rita, to tell her we found her and she's not alone. Tomorrow's visit will be a birthday celebration, so we need a cake, presents, and music, Felice?" He nodded to his sister. "The asylum knows we're coming, and how wonderful to show Rita our loving support."

"You women don't consider how we men live. I have work tomorrow." Albert said.

"As do I, Albert." Marietta said.

"Never fear, we will bring back a thorough report for you, Albert." Felice said.

"Remember the story of the prodigal son?" Cara said. "Welcomed home with opened arms by his father, forgiven all, and reinstated in his family?" She looked directly at Albert.

"My beautiful sister, Camila, do we really think Rita, beautiful, and so intelligent, is mentally crippled and beyond our help? She has been traumatized by both the Rat and now this asylum. But I think she can recover with our help." Dona, said.

Paulo put his crutches under his strong arms and pulled himself up to his full six-foot height. "I am your brother, the same as you. And you don't treat me any differently. That is what Papa always said. I don't understand, what makes Rita any different?"

The discussion stopped and the child ran over and put her arms around her Uncle Paulo.

Oscar stood. "Paulo, as usual, you are the great big loving heart of this family." He shook his brother's hand. "Thank you."

"In the capable hands of Professor Sigerson what seems astronomical for us, is a simple task." He gestured to Rachel, Marietta, and himself. "We need your support to help him bring Rita safely home." He looked around the table. "They call them asylums but they are still madhouses. I would want to be rescued if I were put in a place like that. And this is just what our *famiglia* is for, to keep us safe."

Marietta patted Oscar on the back. "Well said. Paulo, Oscar, Felice, Rachel and I have voted; let's hear from the rest of you. Thumbs up or down?"

Everyone but Albert assented.

Oscar looked around at his family. "*Molto buono!* Papa would be proud." He caught Marietta's eye. "This has gone well." She smiled at him. He slapped Albert on the shoulder. "You'll come 'round soon enough, brother. Remember, there are nine of us, Albert. And then there's Rachel, she's another five."

Marietta playfully put her arm around Oscar's waist, and addressed the room. "I am so proud of my *famiglia*. Now, how shall we celebrate Rita's homecoming?"

CHAPTER 13
THE PROBLEM

"Superintendent Dent went through the sitting-room, giving an occasional 'How do you do?' 'How are you to-day?' here and there among the patients. His voice was as cold as the hall, and the patients made no movement to tell him of their sufferings. I asked some of them to tell how they were suffering from the cold and insufficiency of clothing, but they replied that the nurse would beat them if they told."–Nellie Bly. "Ten Days in a Madhouse."

My dear Watson,

Marcello described last night's dinner as pure theatre: a protagonist, a Greek chorus, music, a hero, a heroine, a villain, and angels. A unique way to make a serious decision, yet in this case it worked exceedingly well. Man's capacity for finding new aspects of his own creativity is always admirable.

This is my first New York day without a clear sky. Today's visit looks to be another improvisational event. In order to inform Miss Rita of our work and her future participation, we are throwing a mock birthday party for her. The theatricality and humour in this moment stands in sharp contrast to the austerity in front of us. Is it whistling in the wind—? I choose to see courage in the face of the unknown.

I have purchased the gift of a soft warm scarf. Two men, three women, and the child comprise the party goers. Felice equates our spontaneous theatrics with minstrel shows or Gilbert and Sullivan, "Where everyone sings very fast" or vaudeville and burlesque comedians, "Who fall on their faces for laughs." Today's birthday party certainly has its comedic possibilities, but also very serious business. I look forward to meeting our heroine and procuring a glimpse of the asylum.

As you know me to be, dear Watson,

Very sincerely yours,
S. H.

We travelled by four-wheeler to Hudson Hospital, full of good cheer and happy anticipation. Felice sang festive songs and Miss Cara joined him. The child was frenzied with excitement to greet her beloved aunt again. Felice, Miss Cara, and Miss Dona were enthusiastic about the commencement of their sister's liberation.

Felice led us in a new song, and we spiralled up Hudson View Drive singing his simple birthday lyric. Nevertheless at the top, we were presented with Hudson Asylum's melancholy bricked building whose gargantuan towers rose above the impenetrable surrounding woodland. I ventured in with my usual formidable energy, accompanied by the Marcello's high spirits. Yet, when we beheld the barred windows and desperate faces within, and heard the screams. It sickened us.

"Mama help me!"

"Get me outta here!"

Thoughts of the punitive abominations of my native Bedlam arose like bile unbidden. As we approached the imposing façade, we were directed to a small cheery family building nearby. Inside there were photos of the hospital's superintendent: receiving awards, shaking hands with political and entrepreneurial figures, and a large display of the venerated Kirkbride design, artistically arranged on the pastel painted walls. Alcoves with tables, couches and comfortable chairs, skylights and large windows looked out onto the garden. The asylum was beyond our reach this day, but not its effects. Miss Rita met us at the entrance. We hugged hello, hushed instead of the usual exuberant family hugs. Miss Rita was wooden, she pointed to an out-of-the-way table. Presents, a cake, tablecloth, and stemware for Albert's wine were produced. Wine and stemware were churlishly confiscated. The party was to commence with music but Felice had put down his guitar. We heard instead a rumble of distant thunder, tree branches scraped the roof and a man was crying on the other side of the visitor's cottage.

Our purpose at this first visit was to pass along information without alerting the hospital staff, but this proved impossible today. Stretched across the sky, a storm cloud brought an unwelcome darkness.

We shared the building with the Battaglia family. Young Daniel, slight, delicate, dark, also a patient at Hudson was crying, begging his father to get him out. "I am afraid, Papa. It's not safe here!"

The staff was as vigilant as vultures and Miss Rita's fear further muted our hopes for a party. She looked like she'd been in the throes of Dante's hell, was terrified, furtively watchful of the staff, and asked us for little things, like a comb, soap, and food. Her hair was dishevelled, her hands shook, and she was clearly well-sedated.

Miss Rita whispered something unintelligible and fell asleep. This was not a hospital. Miss Marcello's arms were covered with bruises. I feared for her sanity and possibly her life. How would one keep a mental patient safe in a State Asylum? The plan must change dramatically.

Felice was indignant. He stood and moved toward the door. I grabbed his arm, and pulled him back to his chair, whispered. "Control yourself, we are being watched. Just think how your actions will play upon your sister! No, her release must be indisputably planned. Our being here alerts them to the fact that Miss Rita is not alone, we are looking out for her. This will help; we must visit frequently, every day if possible."

Felice patted me on the back, picked up his guitar and began playing. "Silver Threads Among the Gold." Staff members hummed along, I nodded to him and our plan commenced.

The child shook her aunt awake. "Aunt Rita, I would like you to meet my friend, Professor Sigerson."

"My pleasure, sir." Miss Rita said.

Felice softly informed her of our plan. "I will play while we talk to cover our voices. Rita, can you be a lookout to let us know if any doctors or nurses are near? If they are, open a present or talk about the cake, got me?" He winked. She smiled with a slight nod.

The child said. "Professor Sigerson is helping us get you out of here."

"Thank God!" Miss Rita took Miss Cara's hand. "When—?"

"Your trial is in ten days." Miss Dona said.

Miss Rita raised her voice. "Oh, let's open this pretty present." She turned it around, shook it, and opened it to find a warm flannel pyjama gown. "Thank you, Cara." She kissed her sister's cheek.

Dr. Simons, the superintendent of Hudson, swiftly entered the room. His short legs pulled him into the building and his large head was full of the toothy smile that stretched full across it. "Of course this is the Marcello family? Very nice to see such spirited involvement, this is the way forward." He shook hands with Felice and myself, and nodded to her sisters. "You know *Signora* Pinto is a favourite patient of mine." He had a thick upper-class Italian accent, moved with the sureness that only comes from giving orders, but not military. He was assessing us, a very composed character, obviously used to being in control.

"Doctor, the family is rather upset by Miss Rita's condition. What could possibly warrant this treatment?" I said.

"Yes, well, most have difficulty at first. But she is quick and will soon come 'round. So nice to have met you, enjoy your visit, my dear." Simons chucked her under the chin, and with the instancy of a Komodo Dragon on the attack, quickly propelled himself across the room.

"Papa, I don't want to talk to him!" Please take me home!" Daniel exclaimed.

Dr. Simons shook hands with Mr. Battaglia. "Oh, don't worry, they all want to leave at the beginning; just look at Mrs. Pinto. If it were easy, there would be no need for my help, would there? Nothing to worry about, your son will soon find that change is within his power." He listened for a few minutes to the father's concerns, and left exuding a sense of patronizing guardianship. We returned to our purpose.

I nodded to Felice, who played his guitar as Miss Dona broke the silence. "You will be examined by two of the asylum's doctors, to prove you are not insane. Just be yourself and you'll be fine. Professor Sigerson is searching for a good doctor to help with the trial."

"Aunt Marietta and Professor Sigerson will be here for you at the doctor's exam. She will bring a suit for you to wear." The child said.

Felice strummed louder. "For she's a jolly good fellow and so say all of us."

When the song died down, Miss Rita nodded to the passing nurse, and Felice began another song. The light that streamed in was shivered by swiftly moving clouds and swaying tree branches where birds were tentatively announcing the coming storm.

"I hope you are keeping yourself safe." I said.

"I am being threatened. I will probably be drugged or maybe restrained after this meeting, but Nurse Nancy will get me out of it and I'll sleep it off. I follow the steps laid out for me." She grabbed my hand. "I am the ideal patient you understand, but this place is terrifying, and what's worse is I don't know where it comes from. Superintendent Simons has a brother, they are both doctors here. His brother scares me. He's involved in everything and so quiet. You know how a crocodile lies completely still under the water for an animal to come to drink or a villager to fish? Then with lightning speed it bites into its prey and the way its teeth and jaw are arranged, there is no way out. The prey is slowly dragged under. I feel like the thirsty prey that can't see what's underwater." Miss Rita said.

Miss Dona took her sister's hands. "Rita, we want you to come home. We will hire the best lawyer to represent you." A dark cloud moved above us to transform the visitor's cottage into one of shadows. "We are all counting on you."

"This is the best birthday gift I could receive." She then picked up another present. "Oh, I wonder what's in this one?" she said loudly, as an orderly stood behind us. She opened it and found my scarf. "Thank you." She nodded to me. "It's so soft." She wrapped it around her neck.

"Enjoy it in good health." I said.

Miss Dona brought out the cake and passed servings around, but the orderly confiscated the candles and the matches. We all had a piece and Miss Rita finished it. The child offered a piece to the nosey orderly, who left.

Miss Cara said. "Has the hospital staff said anything to you about this?"

"No, I didn't find out you were visiting today until the last minute."

"We will do what we can from outside." Felice said below the music. "Sigerson tracked you down for us. Your rescue will come when the legal process is done. Let's celebrate. Have you heard this one?" He began: "Happy birthday to you." Hidden by the song, I questioned Miss Rita.

"Miss Marcello, what can we do to keep you safe?"

"I don't know. I'm in the belly of a shark, and it's filled with demons and few to trust. Nurse Nancy helps people. You might want to talk with her."

"Would it help to have money to buy safety from the staff, or items to barter for your own room or similar considerations?"

"No, they'd just take it as they will these gifts. Get me out as soon as you can."

"Keep alert! Trust your keen mind. Know you are not alone, and stay close to Nurse Nancy." I said.

"Aunt Rita, you focus on the exam. We'll take care of the rest." The child said.

"Rachel, I believe you could."

Thunder again rumbled, lightning showed in a darkening sky, a horse screamed, the wind picked up, tree branches whipped at the skylights. "It's time to go. I'm sorry. I hate to think of you in this place." Miss Cara gave Rita her comb and brush, some hair ribbons. We exchanged hugs, but no goodbyes. "See you soon, Rita."

"Thank you for all your gifts." She looked to me with an anxious smile, and went inside. The cabbie was settling his horse when we filed into the four-wheeler. They held hands. Miss Cara and the child whimpered in each other's arms. As I got in, I called, "Perry Street, cabbie!"

Felice quietly played his guitar. "Professor thank you for stopping my foolish mistake. That was the Mad Hatter's Tea, an un-birthday party, but I'm more worried than before. Rita is fearless and able, yet here she is face-to-face with terror of the worst kind! What can we do?"

"Marcello, your music made it possible. Your sister doesn't know where this evil emanates from. She mentioned Simons' brother, and I will look into both of them." All eyes were on me now. "But wherever this malfeasance originates, they have the complete run of Hudson. None but the patients know what is happening there, and they are silent. This person or system of corruption is protected by much more than the cleverly erected tons of brick that is Hudson Asylum. The whole State Medical, Lunacy, and Justice Systems uphold it. How can we confront that Goliath?"

Miss Dona said. "Isn't that far beyond our aim, professor? What can we do to help Rita?"

"We do what we can, Miss Marcello. Considering her simple requests, I would imagine frequent picnics are a good beginning, also meetings with Simons as often as he requests family attendance. We must assume he wants to help his patients." We approached their home, and they left quietly saying their farewells. Another ripple of thunder was heard.

"Vassar, cabbie." I gently shook my head as we headed north. I thought of Felice's benevolent motto, *Quando il gioco e finite, il re e il pedone vanno nella stessa scatola.* "After the game, the king and the pawn go into the same box."

There had been some gratifying customs acquired during my three-years abroad. The Tibetan practice of meditation was a most welcome addition to my life. The months spent with the teenaged Dalai Lama, my most serene. Meditation happened beyond mind, yet developed mindfulness. The words seemed confusing, but the practice itself was simple. It was of the utmost necessity during those nights I cat-napped in the wilds with my revolver grasped in my hand.

In the quiet of my room, I sat cross-legged in my chair. Once again, I enjoyed the peace and healing of a few moments of serenity. Eyes closed, breathing free of the horror. Yet this horror was nameless, and voiceless, nothing at which to aim my considerable powers. I needed clear data.

Far in the background, the wind and rain increased. I opened my eyes, packed my pipe and began to smoke, sending rings to the ceiling. The problem beat a rhythm in my brain like the terrible threats beating against Miss Rita's very life. And with the heavy humidity of the approaching storm, I abandoned my pipe and succumbed to nightmarish and fitful sleep, filled with Miss Rita's trapped, bruised, and starved face.

    I plummeted into the waterfall and was fighting to breathe. I wrestled awake: "Watson!" The name I called countless ways, the man who completed me, supported me, whom I jettisoned from my life because he was beloved to me and whom Moriarty's ubiquitous henchmen would destroy because of that. There was no Watson here to share the revulsion I felt over this evil day. I am sorry old boy, I thought as I filled and plunged the needle into my arm.

    The storm fast approached, in darkness flashed lightning over the Hudson. My hands found the violin. The music emerged to exorcize the seemingly impenetrable theme of terror that had vanquished my usually polished veneer. Damp, leaden, air shifted as the wind screamed and rattled against my windows. The storm crashed, lightning's frozen images filled the sky, burned my retinas. The music took over. Furiously my tempest-driven improvisations clashed with the lightning, battled with the thunder. I fought the storm from my corner of Main. The wind roared as my music fought through the darkness. Deluge poured over the eyes of my windows, thunder smashed through my attempts, lightning cracked and torched a tree by the Gatehouse. Yet it was my violin that caught fire. Again and again I rose to the call. My strings sang my soul's purpose. The rain splashed over the piers with a disregard for their manmade form, and threatened each moored ship. It formed swift rivulets in the ice, flooding the river area. Deafening thunder reverberated off the mountains, clouds alight with instant daylight. The storm outlasted me. I broke a string, then another as it lashed and buffeted the river town.

The problem was no longer logical: Who was the king and who the pawn? And how could I identify them without knowing their moves? Its solution needed significant modification. My mind was full of the illimitable facts that make my problem-solving abilities so singular. Yet, even I must restring my violin occasionally. This fact alone was uppermost in my mind: One unaided individual could not stand against the enormous dark power of the Hudson River State Hospital for the Insane. Not even Sherlock Holmes.

And with the rain now falling steadily and peacefully as it probably was on Baker Street, exhausted and with thoughts of Dr. and Mrs. Watson sharing the warmth of their hearth fire, I collapsed into sleep.

CHAPTER 14
FIXING THE NETS

"I proceed, Gentlemen, briefly to call your attention to the present state of Insane Persons confined within this Commonwealth. . . I have seen blows inflicted, both passionately and repeatedly… but I have been told that this most calamitous overthrow of reason, often is the result of a life of sin; it is sometimes, but rarely, added, they must take the consequences; they deserve no better care!"–"I Tell What I Have Seen: The Reports of Asylum Reformer Dorothea Dix."

My dear Watson,

I have met my true client. Neither Miss Rita Marcello's intelligence nor her humour has been marred by her three weeks in that asylum. At the time, we were being observed by spies in an enemy's territory. Felice's creation of a musical charade allowed our discussion of the serious issues ahead to proceed. Today, my task is finding a good doctor and you know how skilled I am at that.

My dear fellow, I have despaired over how I would reacquaint myself with a normal life after those dreadful years. My fighting and aim have sharpened to a point, and I heartily find, so are my intuition and deductive skill. My revolver is locked away in my bedroom, old boy, and logic prevails.

Please give my kind wishes to your sweet Mary. I am exceedingly grateful for her care of my most dear friend at this time in our lives.

As you know me to be, dear Watson,
Very truly yours,
S. H.

Early on the morning of March 12, costumed as an old man: with a large brimmed hat, spectacles, beard, cane, shoulders stooped, and my voice the higher timbre of the elder. I began my investigation for collaborators and inquired of the entrance nurse at Vassar Brothers Hospital. "I wonder if you could help me, madam. My granddaughter is acting strangely and has me worried."

Dressed in her school uniform, the child staggered around like a drunken elf. She expounded at breakneck speed: "Oysters, prehistoric oysters, six million oysters, thorny oysters, prolific, windowpane, do they have windows?"

The nurse answered. "I'll call a doctor. Please take a seat."

"Yes, thank you, madam." I questioned her further. "Actually, I was wondering if from your own considerable experience, madam, you would know of a good doctor working also in private practice, who could administer her care at home." My face earnest, "We return to England at the end of the week, madam. In less than a fortnight, she will be back in the capable hands of the inestimable Dr. Moore' Agar."

"I know of two such doctors, Philips and Schwartz. Sir, please come into the consulting room. Dr. Young will see you now." The nurse said.

We stood at his door, Dr. Young sat at his desk with his back to us, reading the note the nurse had handed him. "Sir what is your name?" He wrote it down. "Mr. Newton. Hudson Hospital will be able to help your daughter. My fee for this is $100."

This was all wrong. No recognition, no interest at all, had not greeted us, hadn't looked at the child once. He was slovenly dressed underneath his medical jacket, voice flat, bored. Did Pinto bring Miss Rita through this door? He was putting the child in Hudson Hospital without even looking at her, incorrigible lout! The child endangered here, fool, act now, Holmes!

I quickly pushed her out the door. "Get out, go now!" She left shaken, but fast. And I called to the nurse. "Take my granddaughter to Dr. Philips' waiting room, please madam." I watched them walk down the hall and enter another office. "Thank you."

I rounded on Dr. Young. "Have you ever been to that asylum, sir? You can rip up that admissions form, don't bother, I'll do it for you." I grabbed it off his desk, tore it up and threw it in the fireplace before he could object.

Once again I returned to the character of a befuddled old man. "There must be some mistake. Why don't people listen to me? I'm here for the dentist, sir." I held my jaw in my hand. "You are obviously not that. By the way, did you commit a young woman, Mrs. Rita Pinto to Hudson Hospital three weeks ago, sir?"

"Italians, the pretty one with the cheap husband?"

"Yes, do you recall his reasons, sir?"

"Who are you to ask these questions?"

"Just an old grandfather, sir, I thought her family would like to know. Also, would it be possible for you to write a letter rescinding your judgement that day? Sir, her family wishes to bring her home."

"Mr. Newton, are they doctors?"

"Sir, sir, sir, they would take her to a good doctor if you would write it." He waved me away as if I were a gnat buzzing his ear.

I checked the fire and with his poker made sure the admissions form was a cinder, and went out to the nurse. "Dr. Philips, madam?"

"Yes he is in his office now, come with me. Dr. Philips, will be with you in a minute."

I bent down to look into the child's eyes and gently put my hand on her shoulder, and whispered. "May we proceed?" She exhaled and took my hand in reply.

Philips ushered us into his consulting room. "Dr. Philips, let it be clear we are not interested in anything Hudson Asylum has to offer, sir." I smiled enigmatically, showing my elder's discoloured teeth, and nodded to the child. She bravely went into her act.

The doctor nodded to me and observed her for a few moments.

"There are saddle oysters, wild oysters, seed oysters filling the ocean floor, six million oysters today, and six million tomorrow. Oysters cooked alive, eaten alive. It's horrible." She said.

I deciphered his body language with extreme care. Philips glanced at me, and I could see he was trying to place me. As he continued to watch the child, his face cleared and he smiled slightly. He was coming to the realization that this small piece of theatre was created for him. He clearly saw the humour in it, was close to uncovering us, yet was curious. I relaxed my vigilance.

"So what is the matter here? Your granddaughter is presenting some very serious symptoms, and I don't usually see them in someone so young. She's twelve?"

I nodded minimally. Philips was showing himself to be an open-minded and gentle practitioner.

"Other than the high level of fear she is experiencing." Dr. Philips said. "Normally, I'd say take her home and put her to bed. She will be sober by tomorrow. But in this case, I'd say you'd better put a lock on your liqueur cabinet, Mr.—?"

I cackled, stood up straight, pulled off the hat and beard, and put out my hand, "Professor Sigerson." The doctor smiled and shook my hand. "Dr. Philips, it is time to bring you into our confidence, as it is clear that our little plan was successful. This child is not my granddaughter, but my client, Miss Marcello." She bowed. "With the assistance of Dr. Young, her aunt has been wrongfully committed to the Hudson Asylum by her cruel and violent husband. We have joined forces to release her from this confinement, and are eager to enlist a doctor who can treat her privately. Then we will deliver her to you for evaluation. What do you say?"

"Please, doctor, she is a wonderful person and doesn't need to be in a hospital. Her only problem is the Rat she married. Please help my aunt to be free again, I miss her." The child said.

"You have quickly regained your senses." Dr. Philips said. She smiled. "Of course, I will evaluate your aunt and her treatment. But to remove her permanently, you must prove to me, the hospital, and the state that you have the authority to do so. Will her family back this up? You will also need legal help, as the court oversees her evaluation and removal from the asylum, especially if the husband gets involved."

"Thank you, doctor. He utilized her incarceration to annul their marriage. Will a sibling's authority be sufficient?"

"Yes, she is lucky to have such advocates and has certainly been through enough. The annulment disavows her husband's rights in the case. This is a happy break for her."

"Aunt Marietta was right!" The girl said.

"And would you be able to recommend a lawyer who might have experience with these cases?"

"Morris Henry is a good man."

"Dr. Philips, while you were evaluating the child. I was appraising you. You are an intelligent, compassionate, knowledgeable, and open-minded doctor. Who believes in listening to what your patients have to say. You clearly care about people. Don't mind having a practical joke played on you. Play tennis rather well, and by the casual dress beneath the white jacket of your

111

profession, like to be comfortable, and are a recently married man. A doctor who carries kindness in his bag, as a first and last resort, I trust you will be the physician for Miss Rita Marcello. You will certainly be different from the jailors she has experienced at the Asylum."

"That was perceptive, Mr. Sigerson. How—?"

"That shiny new ring, you are right-handed and favouring that elbow. One must play a lot of tennis to achieve that injury. And the rest, from the way you realized our little joke, plus your treatment of the child, doctor."

"Miss Marcello, have you recently composed a school paper on molluscs?" Philips said.

"However did you guess, doctor? I got an 'A' on it, too."

"I imagine that is an easy grade for you."

"We will not take up more of your time. Thank you, doctor." I shook Philips' hand.

"Thank you, doctor." The child shook his hand hard.

I reapplied my beard and hat, and we left the hospital for a cab. "There's nothing like a little drama to quickly expose the truth, eh, child?" We travelled across town to our respective classrooms.

CHAPTER 15
TRUE AMERICAN REVOLUTIONARIES

"He used to make merry over the cleverness of women, but I have not heard him do it of late."–Dr. John H. Watson. "A Scandal in Bohemia."

Vassar and Poughkeepsie were being acutely tested by an influx of suffragists for two days of meetings and speakers. Topping the bill was the infamous team of Mrs. Elizabeth Cady Stanton and Miss Susan B. Anthony. Even my sanctuary had been disrupted, though in the most genteel way. Professor van Ingen, the Dutch landscape painter boards with me. Most of the scholars were doubling up. Nevertheless, the hallways were crowded, and we few of the male persuasion had even given up our smoking room. For the interim my classes were held in the Observatory's peaceful atmosphere.

I rushed up the stone steps and the two rows of metal stairs through Thompson Library to the Rose Parlour, and ran in through the French doors. My rooms were located on the second floor, and I moved frequently through the suffragists' nerve central. I was bewildered at the interest in this cause and the hundreds of women who lined the halls, cramped the stairwells, and filled to overflowing the Vallard and Faculty dining rooms. Breaking bread in my shared rooms was preferable. I quickly dressed in my robes, gathered my notes.

I raced to class, my robes flying, arms filled with pillows. I headed to the Observatory down the long deep wood-panelled hallway to the stairs. The class had been discussing my treatise on life in the cloistered Tibetan Monastery. Today I hoped to lead them in their first meditation. Miss Anthony appeared from nowhere and pushed Mrs. Stanton's wheelchair directly into my path. I could not slow fast enough and the pillows and their feathers fell around my rather undignified position on the floor. "Tar first, then feathers, professor!" Mrs. Stanton said and Miss Anthony burst into laughter.

I gathered the pillows and rushed down the stairs, handing them off to a student. I lit my pipe as I walked the path to this unique building and ran up the stairway. My students stood at my arrival and I sat them on pillows on the circular floor of the Observatory. Then I scientifically introduced them to an inner exploration.

After class I encountered my famed nemeses again. "Professor 'Feathers,' I don't think you have that gown quite right. Imagine if you had to lace up a whalebone corset, petticoats, and hoops beneath?" Miss Anthony said.

Mrs. Stanton said. "On him the laces would go around twice." They laughed.

"This conversation is beneath you!" I said. "And do you actually believe that women will use the vote to put an end to war, as you have written, madam? I find most women are more interested in a spring hat than in reading the headlines of a newspaper."

"Oh, Professor 'Feathers' has read my article! I'm honoured, sir. Could I be allowed to reciprocate and attend one of your lectures? I couldn't sleep last night and heard your most recent one had the whole class snoring!" They laughed.

"Laugh, Madam, it is because of meditation and not chivalry, that I don't reciprocate your sentiments! The name is Sigerson, I teach anthropology!"

She lowered her voice to an audible whisper. "Professor, was it enjoyable living in the Persian harem, and how much did you pay the husband to get in?" Mrs. Stanton said.

"Those women's lives are desperate. Their fate and that of their children are at the whim of their polygamous husbands. If you had read the whole of it you would know I was there to study and to offer help also. You may want to study it yourselves. Good night."

I retired to my room, where I enjoyed improvising to "Bach's A minor." His mathematical orderliness and grace brought me right. Thankfully, Professor van Ingen rolled in a cart and we discussed the suffragists. He surprised me by his hearty support and a cogent explanation as to why an open-minded, intelligent, bohemian gentleman like himself would do so. He worried for his students graduating into a world without human rights for women. I had to admit I shared his apprehension.

We then happily deliberated over American and European art through supper. Principally the Hudson River School, which was represented in Vassar's Gallery, wisely located next to the chapel. I shared my experiences in Florence with an appreciation of Michelangelo's sculptural work and he said. "Remember what Michelangelo said, 'Beauty is the purgation of superfluities." I heartily agreed. A pipe and brandy gave us a few minutes of quiet repose as Main came to rest after another assiduous day.

Tuesday dawned cold and bright, and Vassar's bellicose infestation would be relieved by the end of the day. I escaped off campus as the child and I breakfasted at the Derby Restaurant. I scowled, "Who taught you to tie a Windsor knot?" She was wearing jacket and tie over her skirt, and purple, white, and gold ribbons pinned to her lapel. She untied it and followed my mimed lesson.

"Aunt Rita took me to Seneca Falls where we met Mrs. Stanton and Miss Anthony. And now they're here just when we need them! Mrs. Stanton is my heroine. Oh, I've brought you some of her writings, from the *National Bulletin*, the *Revolution* and the *New York Tribune*. Please be careful with them, they are important to me."

"And you think these women can assist us with your aunt's removal!"

"They've done it before. They freed a woman in Philadelphia. Hester Vaughn, a domestic, sentenced to death, they saved her life. But all I can think about is what's happening to Aunt Rita, right now!"

"That is laudable, thank you child." I knew I could not accomplish this alone, and those women would enjoy knowing it. Miss Rita's problem required a somewhat different focus, and one I frequently dismissed. Nonetheless, this is vanity; all that mattered was the solution of this case. If they possessed this knowledge of local law and how to successfully circumvent it I'd be an utter fool not to involve them.

Signs posted around town about today's speakers led people to Vassar. We left the carriage, and the child pulled me to the entrance. My intention had been to spend this day away from the uproar and so entered unhappily. Women attired like the child welcomed us inside. We walked through the large arched doorway of the comfortable Rose Parlour, usually so full of students at tea. Like every other room, it had been refitted for this event. An enormous table on the left side, filled with signs and banners, used china, stuffed chairs all around. In two of those chairs, relaxed and sipping coffee, were my tormenters.

Rachel ran over and hugged Mrs. Stanton. "Welcome to Poughkeepsie." She beamed. "Professor Sigerson, meet the greatest women of our day, Mrs. Stanton and Miss Anthony."

"We have already had the pleasure." Mrs. Stanton said icily.

"I have spent many happy hours in this room, debating with my intelligent students." I walked its length and surveyed it with the mind of the only independent consulting detective and ticked off my findings: "Windows unlocked, no guards, open doors, no visible weapons, and far from escape." I turned toward them calmly. "If I were an assassin, you would both be dead. It is too easy to get to you, and there are no checks and balances here. Aren't you afraid someone might act on those death threats I know you receive?"

Mrs. Stanton rang the bell pull. Susan B. Anthony positioned herself between Mrs. Stanton and me. "Are you pronouncing judgment on us or are you going to shoot us, professor?"

"I will not let some misogynistic letters affect how I live my life!" Mrs. Stanton said.

A large gentleman rushed in and grabbed me in a lock hold. "My dear, ladies, you misunderstand my motives, I merely want to open your eyes to the peril you are in. Please disimprison me." I attempted to free myself, testing unsuccessfully one release after another. They both laughed heartily.

I promptly slammed my head back into my attacker's nose, while at the same time, knocking him down by a dislodging of his feet, I held his arm behind his back, and put my gun to his head. "You can be assured that in reality, this gentleman would walk in here and find two dead bodies and an open doorway to the library."

Miss Anthony dismissed their would-be rescuer. "Thank you, Andrew that will be all. Doctor Thelberg's surgery is on the fourth floor should you need her attentions. Professor please pocket your gun!"

"He is impressive, but slow." I brushed off my clothes and straightened my cuffs. "Yet, I am here by merit of the child's belief that you may be of assistance in our quest to free one damsel, Miss Rita Marcello, from the horror of the Hudson Asylum."

"Oh no. Not Miss Rita!" Mrs. Stanton said.

"We've got to get her out right away; it is horrible. She's starving and has bruises on her arms and her hair is a mess, they won't even give her a comb!" The child said.

"I'm so sorry Miss Marcello is in peril. We will do what we can to help you, Miss Rachel." Mrs. Stanton patted her hand.

"Professor Sigerson, you speak of one damsel, do you not see the need for justice in the lives of the women all around you?" Miss Anthony said.

I lit a cigarette and blew the smoke above us. "Ladies are conniving, manipulate their way out of problems, and expect special treatment. Their decisions are affected by trivialities. How can one trust such a quagmire?"

"We have done a superior job of just that. Only the quagmire we have built over and above is the dense impenetrability of the male mind." Mrs. Stanton said.

I waved it away, "I don't doubt your abilities; I doubt your reasoning."

"Professor, you think women are frivolous and scheming, yet you are about to save one, the gentleman to the rescue. It's astounding that with your experiences, the articles you've written which offer hope to women, you are still so blind to us." Mrs. Stanton said.

"Ah, you finished my article, thank you. You ask me to draw a parallel with New Women's lives. But this comparison is a false one and beside the point."

"There are others in that hospital who need to be rescued, yet you are heedless to their plight." Miss Anthony said.

"I am most aware that one man against that fortress is doomed to failure." I stubbed out my fag.

Miss Anthony patted Mrs. Stanton's shoulder. "Now, we know where we stand. Your thoughts are not new to us. Yet your pugilist tendencies may come in handy in this rescue." Mrs. Stanton laughed. "I think the next conversation will be about a way to help Miss Marcello."

"Thank you, Miss Anthony." The child said.

"I have some thoughts on that and will continue this conversation after Mrs. Stanton's speech this evening. Thank you for adding zest to it. We look forward to your participation, professor. We'll see you at seven p.m.? Come, Miss Rachel, join us." Miss Anthony wheeled Mrs. Stanton's chair toward the Assembly Hall. The child waved and ran out.

I leaned back in my chair, lit a cigarette, and growled. "These ladies!" The thought arose with my smoke rings that in order to beat Mrs. Stanton, it was necessary to attend her speech. My violin called me to my room, but anger cannot hold a bow. They are pertinacious yet their assistance could secure my goal. I filled and lit my pipe and smoked, sprawled comfortably on my bed. Looking for fatal flaws, I picked up one of the newspapers the child had given me and casually read Mrs. Stanton's words.

Opening my eyes to darkness, I looked at my watch and bolted out the door. I entered into the large hall stuffed with eager suffragists and sat cross-legged on the wooden aisle floor. I listened eyes-closed with the cool mind of Sherlock Holmes. As I searched for the clues to bring her down, I received only further confirmation of what I had deciphered in the child's newspapers. Mrs. Stanton was exceptionally quick-witted. I shook that from my mind and analysed her statements.

I opened my eyes and watched her. She had come alive, moved about the stage lifted by her beliefs. She was compelling and witty and she was advocating revolution. She herself was a revolution within a revolution. Her quick mind had traced where this suffragist movement would lead and she was taking us there. Each word brought me to the realization that I was unquestionably confronted by a kindred soul. That she was a champion of her day was undeniable.

Nevertheless, I did not like where this led me, to question my assumptions about women? All my experience was against it. Yet here were two brilliant and extraordinary women, rather like my Vassar acquaintances. They're friendship had shaken the very foundations of the world, and mine. I could no longer deny my prejudice, as I now knew it to be. "It is better to learn wisdom late, than never to learn it at all."

I stood, and theatrically bowed to her, then went about quieting her hecklers.

Mrs. Stanton continued: "We are assembled to protest against a form of government, existing without the consent of the governed–to declare our right to be free as man is free, to be represented in the government which we are taxed to support, to have such disgraceful laws as give man the power to chastise and imprison his wife, to take the wages which she earns, the property which she inherits, and in case of separation, the children of her love; laws which make her the mere dependent on his bounty . . . There can be no true dignity or independence where there is subordination to the absolute will of another, no happiness without freedom."

After her speech, I invited them to share a quiet supper with us and to bury the hatchet after their long day.

While their final meeting was in session, I visited the Morgan House Restaurant, and structured a cold repast for their immediate refreshment, a bottle of wine, and prepared the tea when I returned to the Rose Parlour. One could almost hear the building's sigh of relief as Main regained its dignity after the purgation of its superfluities. Teachers moved back into their own apartments to prepare for Wednesday's sessions. I knew tomorrow's classes would invariably include today's focus and looked forward to the duels.

When the child returned, she talked endlessly about her day. "It was amazing. So many people were discussing women's suffrage, and me, too. I was handing out pamphlets and collecting addresses for Miss Anthony and Mrs. Stanton. This must be heaven!"

She ushered in our guests. Our meal began, and I opened the wine for Mrs. Stanton and myself and the child poured tea for herself and Miss Anthony.

Prejudice can cripple; so many women in my cases had been seen as distractions or were left out of the equation entirely. How expeditiously would I have discovered Boone's true identity if I had trusted Mrs. St. Clair's story? Interviewing Miss Harrison could have safeguarded the treaty. What of my conduct concerning the matter of the beautiful Miss Adler? No, this essential diversification unlocked compelling doors for me.

My blinders off, I found in Miss Anthony, a mind used to taking charge, who shared the indomitable fearlessness of the brilliant and passionate Mrs. Stanton. Their strong friendship forged in a lifetime of shared battle was clear. "Please forgive my earlier foolishness. You unmasked my prejudice and this new skin is somewhat tender. But, 'Feathers' was beneath you."

"We get so tired of that pedestal, and do cut ourselves down, usually with Mrs. Stanton's incorrigible humour. I am sorry you got caught up in it, but your long legs entangled in the dress and the feathers in your hair were so funny." Miss Anthony said.

"Child, did you think my enlightenment would result just from our meeting?" I said.

"It didn't take me so long!" She said and slathered mustard on her cold beef.

"I recognized our kinship immediately listening to your speech, Mrs. Stanton." Her blue eyes smiled up at me. "True justice is also my life's quest. You have forced my world open like a clammer with his knife going at one with muscles dead set against opening. You have burst open the very infrastructure of my life and profession to include women in the equation. This decision may prove to be perilous for a confirmed bachelor." Mrs. Stanton laughed.

Miss Anthony patted her hand and said. "Mrs. Stanton, as always, your words are magical."

"Ah, but it takes a mind capable of hearing them. When did you realize your mistake?" Mrs. Stanton said.

"I acquiesced completely at, 'Moral beings can only judge of others by themselves–the moment they give a different nature to any of their own kind they utterly fail.' Your language is supreme, madam."

"It didn't take you very long, professor." said Mrs. Stanton. "Many brave men have supported us from the beginning, but you have to come to your own edification." She smiled.

"My overwhelming focus is the Hudson Asylum and a woman held against her will for three weeks." I nodded sideways to the child.

"And I acknowledge that a fortuitous providence has brought us together."

"Extracting a woman from a mental hospital is a delicate matter. The husband's harassment can switch focus onto the rescuers. These asylums are a law unto themselves, little fiefdoms. The state has given them almost total control over the insane. People disappear into them, and we fear for their lives. But as long as the state doesn't have to see it, they're happy." Miss Anthony said.

"He is no longer a concern. We have found a good-hearted doctor, and lawyer. Can you aid me in effecting her successful rescue?"

Miss Anthony said. "If your legal plans fail, are you prepared to spirit her away to another country?" The child gasped. "In this, the courts are not always on the side of the woman. They disrupt or ruin lives on the word of the husband alone."

"Tomorrow I will pose as an orderly to explore the asylum and will be there in three days for her sanity exam."

"Make sure someone knows of your plans for this visit so they can announce your cab has arrived." Miss Anthony said.

"She can travel to London with me, her brother and sister will find family in Italy. Thank you for your wisdom as to my safety."

The child was now overwrought. "No! Aunt Rita must stay here."

I spoke calmly. "That is our ultimate plan, child. But we must have an alternate solution for your aunt's safety. I am glad for Miss Anthony's experience in this, aren't you?"

"Yes, I don't want her in that horrible place. It's just that I'll miss her all over again if she's in Italy."

"Think," I said. "Then you will have two people to visit in Europe." A concerned frown filled her face and she turned away from me.

Miss Anthony patted her hand and offered to testify at Miss Marcello's trial. Mrs. Stanton agreed to take Rita in her New York apartment, right from the asylum. "No matter the time!" Nurse Nancy was Miss Anthony's contact at Hudson. She was a connection for information, help with the rescue, and most especially, safety on the inside for Rita. I resolved to speak with her immediately.

Mrs. Stanton laughed. "Susan, if we could plan on a suffragist march as part of the escape, it would add quite a unique confusion, don't you think? And possibly wake up Poughkeepsie, too? And if Nurse Nancy can help us add to our numbers, we can rescue as many inmates as possible."

"We'll bring jackets, ribbons, sashes, and hats for the escapees." said Miss Anthony.

The child said. "Change clothing in the middle of a march?" The ladies laughed.

"Of course, Miss Rachel, and then we will march to the safety of the Friends Meeting House." Miss Anthony said.

"Then, oh, we must coordinate with Harriet, first. They could stay at former Underground Railroad houses all the way to Canada! We won't need that many, they are practically there already. A great escape!" Mrs. Stanton said.

"Poughkeepsie is 260-miles from the Canadian border and 300-miles from Montreal. Please don't forget the children." The child said.

Miss Anthony said. "Mrs. Stanton, you're magnificent. I will contact Nurse Nancy beforehand, and ask for as many children as she can rescue."

"A delightful disruption and you will carry this off?" I said.

"That's the easy part." She stood. "The Registrar's office is this way?" Miss Anthony said. She strode down the hall to find the telephone.

"How will all these women defrock in public? Surely in our day this is impossible!"

"For a man, yes." Mrs. Stanton said.

"Explain yourself, madam!"

Mrs. Stanton turned to me, rubbed her hands together and chuckled. "Women wear dresses, even in winter. It's easier to pull things up, on and over, professor."

"I see, but surely your procession will be shadowed, how will you safeguard the recently incarcerated, and what of their arrival in Canada?"

"Miss Rachel, thank you for your help today." Mrs. Stanton shook her hand. "Professor, we will contact our Quaker friends in Montreal and they will happily take our refugees in hand. As for shadowing, I imagine that your plan includes the sabotaging of the asylum's means of communication with the outside world?" I smiled my ascent. "Then you should know that the American Suffragists are proud of our record of peaceful protest. The only time a suffragist has been arrested in New York, was when Miss Anthony voted 'illegally.'"

Miss Anthony returned from her phone call. "I will never pay that fine! They thought they were intimidating me. Imbeciles! It was the shot heard around the world! The fools didn't even realize it was our national call to arms. Mrs. Stanton, the word is out; my local cohorts are working on it. They will also get a message to Miss Tubman."

"Once more unto the breach,' my dear, Susan, 'once more." Miss Anthony rubbed Mrs. Stanton's tired shoulders, they smiled.

"When will you leave the asylum?" said Miss Anthony.

"9 a.m."

"Perfect, our march will be there."

"The gates and the asylum doors open at 8 a.m." I pushed plates out of the way and drew a rough map. "The classroom you are interested in is here." I pointed with my cigarette. "I will contribute more detail following my visit. What is your plan?"

"We will march from the Meeting House to the asylum grounds and to an out-building where the women will be waiting."

"Those buildings are here." The child drew an "X" on the drawing.

"Chanting loudly, we will quickly absorb the women and children into our March then pass through Market Street, maybe a speech, Mrs. Stanton? Then return to the Meeting House." Miss Anthony said.

"A well-defined diversion, I will also appeal to the Houdini Brothers for their diabolical amusement of the staff. And will be in my most formidable guise in the main building."

Mrs. Stanton said. "Yes, I think we've had a taste of that, already! Susan, I'm sorry to miss all your fun. I will be at my New York apartment to greet Miss Marcello. But Professor 'Feathers' are you sure there isn't a bit of revolutionary in you?"

"You might want to contribute to the success of these women, and we will be quietly accepting donations." Miss Anthony said.

"Rachel, join us at our next meeting. Or come for a visit, both of you." Mrs. Stanton said.

I contributed a quiet gift from Her Majesty's England, something Mycroft will find quite revolutionary.

In the cab to Perry Street, the child intoned sleepily: "We just had supper with Mrs. Stanton and Miss Anthony, right? And I helped at their suffragist meeting?" She yawned. "And you are really my friend? I'm not dreaming am I?"

"No, but you are rather tired. It was illuminating to be in the presence of true revolutionaries. Thank you."

"You mean after you finished yelling at them?" She laughed.

"They began as intelligent girls who employed their very different geniuses to break through the considerable barriers for women's suffrage. Because they accepted their life's challenge with wit and a most stalwart companionship, your future is bright."

She was strangely quiet. I understood quiet, then she looked up at me. "Professor Sigerson, thank you for helping Aunt Rita, but, do you think you could stay here for a while?"

We arrived at her door, and she walked inside. "Goodnight."

I lit my pipe for the drive back.

My dear Watson,
This case has some rather surprising points of interest. Some of them come from places I have never until now allowed in my life, from those I used to dismiss. I wonder how much more of the world is there, hidden behind fallacious beliefs.
As you know me to be, dear partner,
Very sincerely yours,
S. H.

CHAPTER 16
TWO BROKEN THREADS

"It makes a considerable difference to me, having someone with me on whom I can thoroughly rely."–Dr. John H. Watson. "The Boscombe Valley Mystery."

My dear Watson,

This American journal has shown me how admirable are your writing talents, dear friend. Yet, what foul mood led you to paint me as a "heartless calculating machine?" Nonetheless, when I return, you may find this trip has certainly made some appreciable changes.

For privacy's sake, you must know, I obscured some of my feelings from you, a requirement when living with one's biographer. Yet there were several from our exploits I had feelings for. My keenness concerning Miss Adler I kept from you entirely as I knew it would wind up in the middle of the romantic story you were writing. And where could it have led? Watson, there are some things I do like to keep private.

Two great ladies I have met here have appreciably continued Miss Adler's mind opening endeavours. One is turning ninety while the other would never be interested in my attentions, yet I am grateful to be considered a friend. Together they have realigned the world's axis towards true justice. But you already know the wisdom and power of women, sharing your life with your wonderful wife, Mary.

As you know me to be, dear friend,
Very sincerely yours,
S. H.

It was a singularly agreeable morning as I transported Miss Marietta to Vassar for breakfast in the Faculty Dining Room. Classes had already started and it was fairly empty.

She said. "Next month Vassar will be beautifully in bloom."

"It is perennially in bloom, with the exceptional minds of young ladies who can see beyond what society demands of them." I looked in her eyes and reached for her hand. "And I will miss what I have found here."

The servers took our orders and I poured the coffee.

"Yesterday, Miss Anthony also corroborated your thoughts about the annulment. It is indeed your sister's freedom from Pinto."

"Yes and soon I hope, from that horrible place. There's a question I've been meaning to ask, do you—?" She hesitated a moment and I looked to her. "Do you have anyone special waiting for you in London, professor?"

I dropped the sugar tongs. "I am as unfettered as you are, Miss Marietta. Why do you ask?" Our meal arrived yet we hadn't acknowledged its presence.

"It's a shame such an intelligent, gentleman is alone."

I put down my coffee cup. "It is my choice, my work is supreme." I engaged her beautiful eyes. "But I have noticed that your perfume is one I fancy. And I do look forward to our conversations." She beamed at me and with a laugh we discovered our bangers and eggs.

Later in the privacy of our cab we travelled down Main Street close together and enwrapped in rugs. The Hudson River's icy silver majesty sparkled opal-like ahead of us.

"Miss Marietta, you impress me, and not just how keenly you face your challenges." I nuzzled her hair and she squeezed my hand under the rugs and leaned her head on my shoulder. I kissed her hair. She moved to face me and our lips met in a light kiss, then with more expression to which she responded completely.

"Professor Sigerson, I had no idea."

"Miss Marietta, please, your truthful and direct nature is far above such false pretences."

"Thank you for your complement, I find much to like in your nature also."

"Miss Marietta, my life is centred in London and I will be returning in ten days." I whispered into her hair. "Have you ever imagined living there?"

She sat up. "London? With its horrible fogs, dirty river, constant rain, and streets filled with poor children and such, not for me." She smiled and looked me in the eye. "I dream of sun and warmth, living there you must crave it also, California calls me. I will be joining Oscar at the fair, hopefully Rita will, too."

I sighed, gently moved a wisp of her hair back in place. "Forgive me. There has not been proper time for this. I have been supremely focused on what has turned out to be a considerable enterprise."

"Would you leave London to consider my California dream?"

We right turned into her quaint residential street. Its line of strong, rooted mature oaks led the way to the Marcello's home. We exited the cab.

"Thank you for your company." I kissed her hand. "*Au revoir* and keep warm, Miss Marietta."

I ran up the stairs to Marcello's studio. The child yelled to her uncle. "Sigerson coming up!" Upon entering, I noted his sheepish look. Dusted with plaster, he also seemed frustrated, ill at ease, and had just covered up a tall sculpture. Miss Anthony's attentions toward Mrs. Stanton recalled how I depended upon Watson to be my second set of eyes and dead-eyed shot in dangerous corners. Marcello was doing an excellent job of filling in. I took out a cigarette, lit it, and offered my case to him.

"Marcello, I should be extremely obliged if you would meet me with a cab, beginning Friday, four afternoons at four p.m. at the Hudson River Asylum. Bring your pistol. I will be undercover as an orderly. Upon arrival, keep the cab at the front entrance and immediately announce to the guard at the door that 'Mr. Adam Newton's cab has arrived.' It is absolutely essential that you follow these directions exactly. The consequences are dire: The least being my arrest for much of my plans, and the most, Miss Rita's re-commitment."

"Of course I will, my friend."

"There is one more thing. I have been counselled, if our legal plans break down, to have a hiding place out of the country, for Miss Rita. I can provide transportation to London. But she would need contact with her family in Italy. You or Miss Marietta must find that for her. This information is confidential and only goes to me, no later than the day before her trial."

Marcello looked worried yet nodded. "Surely this won't be needed. It would be so sad for us to lose her again. The suffragettes told you to do it? God, I hope it doesn't come to this!"

"Nevertheless, we must prepare. This is something to keep between the four of us, yes? Sadly, your niece already knows." I put my hand on his shoulder. "Marcello, the woman we saw on Friday, was not the sister you know and love. She was terrified; there were bruises on her arms; she was so drugged she fell asleep, and she asked us for soap, for food. We have to get her out of there immediately, even if that means out of the country."

"My poor sister has suffered enough! I'll find that, Sigerson, immediately. Why is her release taking so long? And what are your plans?"

"The legal process is slow. Ships leave weekly; the last ship I feel I must take leaves port March twenty-fourth that is my point of convergence." If I don't make it back to London, by the end of this month, the commencement of Moriarty's case could be left to that fool Lestrade to bungle! No, it must be then!

"That fits with our Fair plans. Did I hear an alias, Sigerson?"

"Yes, necessary for this rescue. When that dark pandemonium falls, we will be ready." I threw my cigarette to the fireplace.

"You've met with those suffragettes?" He spat out the word, Marcello's anger rose, he pointed his finger in my face. "But, Rita should be your only focus!"

I now realized his agitation was directed at me and kept my voice calm, yet firm. "When we visited Miss Rita, I realized this was much bigger than your sister, Marcello. I suspect several victims. I will know more when I visit tomorrow. Of course Miss Rita is our first priority, but not the only one, and I require competent assistance to accomplish this significant task."

"She should be!"

Quietly. "Marcello, your sister would accept my focus. Have you lost faith in my method, sir?"

He was pacing the studio, like a caged animal. "No, but like Rachel, I'm frustrated."

I waved it away as unimportant. "She's an irresponsible child, man!"

He pushed me. "Irresponsible? Irresponsible! Rachel came home from your recent exploit terrified. I've never seen her so afraid." He threw his cigarette down and crushed it with his boot! "I refuse to allow her to accompany you on any more of these missions." He came at me, grabbed my lapels. "What is wrong with you man, she's a 12-year-old child!" He took a step back and threw a hard right which caught me unawares.

I seized his hand and held it. "That was an exceedingly unfortunate incident of which I am not proud. We inadvertently revealed the evil doorway through which Miss Rita passed. The monster without even looking at the child was dispatching her to the asylum. I sent her to safety, and destroyed the admissions papers. Your niece was exceedingly courageous and continued with our search for a doctor with the qualities we found in Dr. Philips. I understand and laud your protective anger. But we are dependent upon the court's timing. If you want my help, Marcello, you will work with me, and not against me. I am not a novice at this."

"How is that?" He forcefully pulled his hand from mine. "When does living with savages give you experience with the law, with extracting my sister from the horror she lives in and keeping Rachel safe? You've convinced Marietta that you know what you are talking about, but I wonder."

"I will continue with this with or without your approval, Marcello." I moved my jaw, assessing it. "Though, I would rather we worked together, your handling of Pinto during my folly proved your considerable mettle to me." I lit a cigarette, took a long drag. "I owe you better treatment than this. You are not the first to accuse me of keeping my findings too close to the vest. I am sorry if I have left you out in the cold.

"The experience of my explorations included the knowledge of each country's law. Resulting in the negotiation and ending of longstanding feuds and reuniting of family tribes. And the aspect of my recent *National Geographic* article which interests the ladies so: the safe rescue of one woman and her children from the harem. Do you require more?"

"Sigerson, things seem to be getting worse, not better!" He clapped me on the back. "Forgive me. Of course I will continue to work with you." He took out his Colt.

"Marcello, I am a semi-pro bare-knuckled boxer, yet you just clipped me. I'd say you can do more than hold your own in a fight. And I'd clean that where there isn't so much plaster." I patted him on the back, raising a small dust cloud."

"I forget where I am."

"The mark of a true artist is total and complete focus on one's art to the exclusion of all. I consider myself an artist of sorts, you can be sure of my focus, Marcello."

"Yes, or you will spend my afternoon piling on more than enough proof to convince me." We laughed.

"I have heard that before, too. Your niece has a strong advocate in you and I am glad to see that. With her intelligence and the dreams that arise from it, she will need your support in the coming years."

"Of course, I love Rachel, but as my life is fast moving away, my help will not always be here. I worry about her, but she's plucky. As you say, Vassar may be the answer. And she's a girl, what choices does she have above finding the right husband? I have worked long and hard for my career to take off as it seems to be doing."

I gestured to the sculpture with my cigarette. "Is this piece going on the train?" I said.

"It's not important."

I saw the dodge. "Good luck with it. I'll see you Friday, 4 p.m." I shook his hand. "Marcello, I often think of these lines by Thucydides:—'The bravest are surely those who have the clearest vision of what is before them, glory and danger alike, and yet notwithstanding go out to meet it.'"

CHAPTER 17
GREAT ELEMENTAL FORCES OF NATURE

"... dashing in as she had done many a time before, with all the fearlessness of youth, thinking only of her task and how it was to be performed."–Dr. John H. Watson. "A Study in Scarlet."

My dear Watson,

There is a blizzard billowing outside my windows, it's been snowing all night, and there are fourteen and 3/4 inches on the sill. You would probably say:—"Nature's white covering o'er all that is grey, dark and evil, a clean, fresh beginning. A welcome reminder that man's industry is not in charge today. It calls to all ages: 'Put down your work, and play in Grandfather Frost's crystalline celebration!"

It began with a sleigh ride. As you are no doubt aware it is dangerous for me and for all those I have met in Poughkeepsie to be discovered here. To show myself in such a way, and blather on about Persia was foolish. Persia and Tibet were ways to deflect the attentions of Moriarty's assassins, and gifts for Mycroft, nothing more.

As you know me to be, dear fellow,
Very sincerely yours,
S. H.

A snowball smashed into my frost-covered window. I opened it gingerly. Never one to form a sentence with any degree of tact, the child yelled. "Professor, catch!" She threw one at me which hit my chin and melted down the inside of my dressing gown.

"What the devil, child!" I quickly wiped away the snow.

"Oops—sorry!" She held up her embroidered handkerchief.

I dressed, brought hot chocolate, my coffee and brandy flask and joined her in the sleigh.

The snowfall created a carnival atmosphere as each new layer of the magic white surprise had rendered schools and businesses quietly obsolete. It was a welcome change from the darkness that had filled our days of late. Children had escaped from school and were everywhere, the city theirs for a day: engineering forts for snowball wars, calling out as they tobogganed down the long hilly streets, envisioning fairylands in the transformed trees, and building snow creatures everywhere. Schoonmaker Stables pulled out all their sleighs for river rides, their clear bells awakening memories of the Yorkshire countryside.

We joined the others sleighing down river. "Where did you get that hat?"

"It's called a deerstalker, and Uncle Oscar says it's a hunting cap."

"Halloa!" I grabbed it off her head and lobbed it towards New Jersey. It caught the wind and flew out of sight.

"Why did you do that? Now, I'm cold." She leaned back into the furs, arms crossed.

"There are better hats, child." I took off my grey topper and put it on her head.

"This one's warmer, thanks." She looked at me with a question in her eyes. "Sir, I'm in a pickle and need your help."

"I thought as much."

"Would you speak at my school tomorrow? They're having an assembly and I know they would like to hear about your explorations. So would I." She sipped her hot chocolate.

"This is why you invited me into this sleigh. I refuse!"

"But, it would help me out." She said with that pleading look with which children are expert.

"I'm sorry, child, we can talk about Persia anytime. Now, if you'd like?" Our driver turned and we beheld the glittering three-storey icicles hanging from the Palisades cliffs.

"You are being pig-headed!"

"Name-calling never wins out, child. Indeed, it shows a laziness of intellect, which I know not to be true."

"Why won't you?"

Sigh. "I applaud the fact that you have done your best to learn Miss Anthony's negotiating skills, but sometimes the desire to know is best tempered with patience."

She stopped the sleigh on Main Street, jumped out, and threw my hat at me, then joined her tobogganing friends. I went to Hyams store and secured a suitably warm replacement hat for the child, and crossed to the Morgan House tobacconist to purchase necessities. I savoured a warming drink at the bar, and witnessed Pinto as he entered the hotel. He did indeed have friends to be out on bail so soon. Yet it seemed he was still plying his trade as he swaggered over to the hotel manager.

Commendably the manager was not having any of it. "Get out. This is a first-class hotel!"

"It wouldn't be so high and mighty first-class, if it suddenly burnt down, now would it?"

I stood near enough to the manager for Pinto to notice, my jacket casually opened to show the gun in my pocket. Yet, the manager must have attended Harold's meeting, as he quietly placed his Colt on the desk and pointed to the door. "What do you think Inspector MacKinnon will say to that? Get out!"

Pinto departed. I saw the man's pride shine in his eyes as he quietly returned his revolver to its drawer.

I watched Pinto as he ascended Main Street toward Clinton Street. Main was now cleared of snow and the trolleys were running. I called a cab to Vassar. On my way out of town, the snow coloured and sparkled in the golden light of the setting sun. But ahead, it was moving: a scuffle was in progress, three against one! The cabbie reined in the horse sharply. I leapt into the fray. Her shabby clothing, the defiant way she addressed her attackers and her valiant yet calamitous attempts at escape made clear the child was being accosted. One gagged her with his hand, and another spat in her face, the third foully addressed her. It looked as if she had already taken some punishment. Her hair was clotted with snow, and her exposed extremities reddened from the cold. She was fighting back, but three assailants put one in a very dangerous position.

"Stop this immediately!" I pulled them from the child. "Now, sit!" I tied their wrists together sequentially. They would have to work as a team to get home.

I carried her to the cab and piled on the rugs. "Child, are you all right?" She nodded. I rounded on the boys, all six-foot-two of me glaring down at them. "What a nice little gathering of evildoers. I deduce that in a few years if you continue on this trajectory, boys, you will all be behind bars. There is no doubt. Think about it. If that's what you want, keep following this road."

As if conjured, Poughkeepsie's police force appeared and ended Pinto's uphill retreat. He was roughly searched and cuffed. Arrested, and locked in the Black Maria van. The officers took off with their prisoner pleading pitifully for release.

I pointed to the boys. "Today you stand at a threshold in your lives. Choose wisely!"

I examined the child again, she was dangerously cold. "Oh, you've got a blinker. Vassar, Cabbie! If you arrive in five minutes time, I have a silver dollar for you!" I wrapped my scarf around her and crowned her with my hat.

We hastened in, I sent a student to the fourth floor to alert the doctor. In my sitting room, the child washed her face, and dried her hair with a towel. I hung her wet outer clothes to dehydrate by the steam pipes. I settled her in the settee, cocooned in every blanket I had, and mixed her a quarter-shot of brandy with water, which she sipped, but hated and put on a pot of tea.

"Well, I think I've done as well as my doctor friend would."

A knock at the door and I welcomed in Dr. Thelberg. She displayed the competent air of the physician and bore additional blankets. Nonetheless, I was surprised to shake hands with a woman doctor. Like most of the female professor's here, she was a pioneer, the first female doctor in the state of Colorado.

"Professor Sigerson, I hear your lectures are not to be missed. Oh, what do we have here?"

"The child was attacked and beaten by school bullies in the snow a few moments ago. I am a friend of the Marcello family."

"Let's see, excuse me Miss Marcello, may I touch your face?" The child nodded. "Oh, my, my, my, this shouldn't happen; it's not right, just not right. How do you feel?"

"I'm cold and it hurts when you push on it like that, ouch!"

The tea was ready, I added honey.

"Miss Marcello, you have periorbital ecchymosis, contusion around the eye with bruising, discoloration, and swelling. But you must warm up first before applying any ice to your face. Your body will heal itself. To help it along will require ice for two days and then heat. And aspirin for pain, but probably unnecessary in such a healthy child." She picked up the glass, smelled it and handed it to me. "Professor we don't apply brandy to young children. Blankets work well, and make sure her feet and head are covered, and please move her closer to the radiator. I would also bring her home once she has sufficiently warmed."

"Thank you, doctor."

She shook my hand. "Don't hesitate to call me if she doesn't warm adequately or if there are any other changes. Farewell."

"How do you feel, child?" I wrapped her thoroughly in the additional blankets, socks and my scarf.

"Better, the tea is helping. Professor, they were really going to hurt me this time."

"You don't consider that black eye to be serious? So this isn't your first? You set me up! What this day has been all along: An act of persuasion. My public speech would provide a way for your friends to observe your protector and be scared off. Is this correct?"

"I needed your help!"

"Child, you always have my help. You don't need to keep waylaying me. I have grown up with bullies, also. Yet I have much more experience in the world and know its consequences."

"Professor, you wouldn't have understood, no adult does."

"No one forgets what they experienced at an English boarding school, child. Even the best of them are filled with bullies. And no one stops it. It's like a little criminal underworld in every school. It is simple to do. Yet, administrations allow it to go on. They also bully, however—it's criminal. I got out as soon as I could. I had to blow up part of the chemistry lab to do so."

"So that's what I'll do."

"That would ruin your chances with Vassar."

"But, professor—?"

I moved the settee closer to the radiator. "Skipping up will get you there sooner. Are you warming, child? You're half-mourning, I'm afraid." I passed her a mirror.

"But the bullies love to sink their teeth into the smart kids."

"We will find another way to sour the milk."

"How—?"

"Speak with your Uncle Giuseppe. We have conspired to put an end to it."

"How can an old bully teach young bullies to not be bullies?" She yawned.

"Exactly! We are endeavouring to create the first American School of Baritsu boxing at your high school. The key is to involve the bullies in its operation. Thereby imparting defensive skill to the student body and creating an occupation for the bullies. All of it overseen by your uncle."

"Will it work?" She yawned.

"Like a dream." I whispered and caught her tea cup as she nodded off. When she was sufficiently warmed, I hailed a cab to her home. She fell asleep again in my arms. I covered her with another rug, carried her inside to her bed, took her shoes off, added socks, the new hat, and tucked her in. On my way out, I interviewed Miss Cara reading in the sitting room. "Your niece is asleep but still in uniform. She was attacked in the snow by school bullies today, and she suffered from the cold. A few more blankets are a good idea. She will also need ice for that shiner tomorrow."

Miss Cara groaned. "Not again! Poor kid, I'll take care of her. Thank you, sir. I don't think you know how you have affected her life. She turned a corner when she met you. Life has not always been good to her." She shook her head and went to find blankets.

I turned back to her. "Miss Cara, what corner did she turn?"

"She was very young when she lost her parents, as I was. It affects your whole life. She's happy here, but there are the bullies."

"What do you think happened to her parents?"

"I was younger than she is at the time: Maybe an accident?"

"Is there anything else you can tell me?"

"No, we know as little as she does, professor."

"Thank you, Miss Cara, goodnight."

My dear, Watson,

Old fellow, we were becoming two middle-aged bachelors, stuck in our ways together. Your marriage has pulled you out of such stagnation and my joie de vivre *has reawakened in the States.*

No doubt your life with Mrs. Watson awakens wisdom in you every day, and you, dear boy, have always had room in your heart for love. Please thank her for me, for the joy she has brought to my most stalwart friend, my partner in justice.

Imagine my climb to that lofty plateau? It would be my greatest mystery. As the old Greek Stoic put it: "Si vis amari, ama:– – To be loved, love."

As you know me to be, my dear friend,
Very sincerely yours,
S. H.

CHAPTER 18
THE DARKEST HOUR

"Here am I literally entombed alive by fraudulent means, for a wicked purpose, by the despotic will of my husband. My life is almost daily and hourly endangered and I am allowed no communication with the outside world."– Elizabeth Parsons Ware Packard. "The Prisoners' Hidden Life, Or Insane Asylums Unveiled."

My dear Watson,

Having spent a lovely afternoon in the stacks of Vassar's Library, my research proved instructive. Hudson River State Hospital for the Insane opened in 1887 as one of the new facilities adopted throughout the State of New York as asylums. Immediately it applied the fashionable Pinel and Tuke's philosophy of "Moral Treatment." This achieved for the state the consolidation of its mentally imbalanced citizenry, who had gained a refuge from the gutters, jails, and alms-houses.

Sadly, all too soon, this approach failed in the large state institutions. It quickly became a regime of enforced occupational therapy, food austerity and exercise-yards. The workhouses emptied, hospitals and families dumped into the asylums their enfeebled, elderly, and poor. In the resultant overcrowding, morality became obsolete. In the financially driven search for a better method, emergency restraints returned, and superintendents allowed experimental approaches. The inconsistent motives of aiding lunatics and of protecting the community from them conformed all too well to the new theory of eugenics. Purporting that mentally ill people are subhuman and need to be purged from the general population. A classist concept carried to the extreme!

This enormous asylum was built on the popular Kirkbride design as two five-storied, red bricked fortresses with large public spaces, a multitude of outbuildings and classrooms. The imposing facade of this fearsome architecture is perched atop a massive hill, camouflaged with rolling greens and tended gardens. Its coveted view of the Hudson River is breath-taking. From their locked and barred windows, the inhabitants stare wistfully at the river's illusory freedom.

As you know me to be, dear fellow,
Very sincerely yours,
S. H.

> **Help Wanted, Male & Female**
>
> BEGIN a career in Mental Health and receive personal satisfaction, security, good salary, advancement opportunities, liberal fringe benefits. Most positions are for: Psychiatric Attendant or Food Service Worker. High school diploma or experience helpful but not required. Apply at Hudson River State Hospital, Personnel Office, Main Bldg., Poughkeepsie, N. Y. 452-8000.

Mr. Adam Newton had telegraphed Hudson expressing interest in the job. On Friday, I embarked upon my introduction to the asylum as an *employé* and was loudly greeted at the entrance by two policemen wrestling with a screaming patient. One of them called to the attendant at the door. "We got another one, Mac, caught him down by the river trying to hop on a sleigh." Orderlies arrived and stuffed the patient into a straitjacket. They picked him up and carried him, still screaming his anguish and despair. The policeman continued. "He bit poor Fred, on the hand, there. It's all part of the job, right, Fred?"

The nurse addressed him. "Come in, we'll take care of it. Human bites can be nasty. We are a hospital after all."

I coughed. "Where will they take that patient, nurse, what's next for him?"

She turned to me, her face expressed—Not from around here. "I'm sorry, who are you?"

A young doctor pushed in. "Are you Newton?"

"Yes."

"He's here for the orderly job. I'm Dr. Simons. Call me Joey." I entered and shook his hand.

"That was some commotion. Are you called upon to handle such extreme situations on a regular basis?" Dr. Joey was the Superintendent's brother? Was he reliable, a follower, or a henchman, someone not to be trusted? He has an easy-going countenance, mud on his boots, and somewhat intelligent eyes. How can a doctor have dirty fingernails? The way he hefted that screaming patient showed strength, but also an apathetic nature. What else was behind those eyes? Was he under his brother's thumb or was it the other way around?

"Because of my size, I'm always called in to restrain a difficult patient. My duties encompass the whole of Hudson, but this is my least favourite." He looked as if he had swallowed something distasteful.

"Is this a weekly or daily thing?"

"Two or three times a week." Dr. Joey said.

I studied the inside of the bleak building, synchronized it with the map in my mind: Main entrance locked, guarded: Forced exit possible depending upon the guard. There are bars on every window. Patients look disheartened, alone, afraid, sedated, and lost. There are no small groups talking together, no conversation at all. Other exits go out to the garden from the north side of the building.

"Are there any other exits besides those near the garden? Are they locked?"

"No, it's open all day. Everything's locked up at five o'clock. The upper floors are always locked. There are four wards on the first floor, four on the second floor, and one on the third floor, next to the infirmary. The men's ward is located on this side and the female's on the other."

"Thank you, Dr. Simons. I appreciate taking your time." I took out my cigarette case. "May I smoke here?"

"No, the only place to smoke indoors is the orderlies' locker room."

We entered the locker room. "Your uniform put it on."

I hung my coat, and put a match to my cigarette. He lit his pipe and that was all I could get out of him. He withdrew into himself as he smoked. Would he prove to be the man I am searching for?

From the locker room, I walked through cold, dreary corridors into the bright atrium with a view of the snow-covered gardens. Residents read and sat in the light that streamed in through windows and skylights. Behind that image, I observed a high level of palpable fear, despair, fresh knife or nail cuts in various stages of being healed. I recognized bruises purpled on faces, ankles and wrists, hands trapped in gauze, similar to Miss Rita's maltreatment. Shortened hair that had been cut to extremes, or pulled out by inmates doing horrible things to them-selves: I looked into tortured eyes that didn't see me, contorted faces, and drug-hollowed stares, their minds full of nothing, their bodies clenched, cringing at the screams within and around them. The smell of strong disinfectant assaulted the senses. My discriminating hearing pinpointed muffled repetitive, banging coming from the locked wards.

In this enormously overcrowded hospital, some trifles stood out. My attention was drawn by two patients in wheelchairs. One woman extremely distressed expeditiously rolled herself around the room, knocked into others and over feet in her agitated search for a certain lady reading quietly in the sun. She spoke fast-paced gibberish as if her clockwork spring had been over-wound. Every muscle of her face expressed intense emotion and worry. Yet, her words were unintelligible. The woman she had anxiously sought answered her clear as a bell. "That must have been hard to do." The other exploded in happy gibberish, her face relaxed. She smiled, and patted the other's hand, calming the wordless.

As I headed out the door, I searched for Dr. Joey and found him in the Conservatory. Bundled up in sweaters, wearing a flap cap, his hands in gloves with fingers freed to sift the dirt and an intense look on his face as he potted a seedling. "This will become part of daffodil hill." He said with pride in his voice.

"How about taking me on that tour?"

We walked out and behind the asylum building. I lit a cigarette and drew the map on my shirt cuff. "You can see the new Edgewood buildings, the visitor's building, laundry and tailor shop, carpenter shop, classrooms and the School of Nursing. Everything opened at eight a.m." He paused between thoughts, stopped, and looked at his watch.

I opened the door of the nearest classroom, nodded to the teacher, said. *"Bonjour!"* Most of the students looked cold and bored. After answering me the teacher continued with a very basic French lesson. Yet, in the back Rita was staring at me, smiling she pantomimed twirling a moustache. I tipped my hat, and left before our exchange was noticed.

"The south wing is this way." Dr. Joey said.

"What time of day is it in operation?"

"Anytime." He shrugged. "Herman's always tinkering with his new electrotherapy batteries."

We went down two levels in a large hydraulic lift that opened into an ample, concrete sub-basement area. He lit a lamp. The light showed that it inhabited half of the building area above it, divided up into a succession of rooms with white-tiled walls and floors. Observation windows on each door faced the hallway. The therapeutic facility was empty, the air full of fresh hygienic solution.

Dr. Joey rattled this off in a flat tone: "Above us is our kitchen on the first basement level. On this level are sound-proofed seclusion cells with padded walls and floors. The electrotherapy rooms, and force-feeding stations equipped with restraint beds. The operating theatre for psychosurgery, hysterectomy and male or female castration: The bathing area and Bath of Surprise for cold water shock." He abruptly stopped.

"It's called 'bath of surprise?" I smiled. The room had multiple drains in the floor. A ladder led up to a ten foot high wooden box frame with a trapdoor lid, like a gallows. Below it was the ice cold bath.

"It can stop a heart." He said.

Add to my inner map: Two ways in or out, lift required an operator, and stairs. There were no other exits: no windows, no pillows, no blankets, and no towels. These empty torture chambers, how can one think of them any other way? I envisioned the slammed doors of padded cells, the unacknowledged pleas. The snap of manacles onto innocent hands and feet, the terrible jolts of electricity, and the surgeon's scalpel as it cut irretrievably into brain or womb filled me with apprehension and dread.

"Is there a way to turn the electricity on, here in this room?"

We walked over to an electrics room, and he demonstrated. "Yes I think Herman is working on that. We have six of Dr. Stohrer's Dresden double batteries they can each increase to 150 milli-amperes of electricity. Positive pole electrodes are applied to the head. Basins of acidulated water for the feet and by having both hands and feet in the water it is possible to send a current up or down both extremities and the spine at the same time."

We ascended as we came. "How does one acquire the idea that the body of a mentally ill person is fodder for experimentation?"

Dr. Joey shook his head.

"Thank you. When do I start, and the pay is $28.00 a month?" I said.

"Tomorrow at 8 a.m." He turned away.

I called after him. "See you then. Good afternoon."

Marcello arrived, and I cabbed to my class at Vassar pondering Dr. Joey's eccentricities.

Saturday became my first day of official employment at Hudson. The Simons brother's perplexities were still to be solved. I looked forward to weekend quiet and the chance to interview the inhabitants.

While on duty in the atrium, I observed a young woman, Miss Helena, dressed like a suffragist in long skirt and man's jacket, she was speaking to a small group of inmates. They were looking around, biting their nails, pulling their hair, and bouncing up and down in their chairs. She spoke with the attitude of a preacher. "Can flesh-and-blood people just disappear? Who is buried in unmarked graves? I don't know but I know where they are." She pointed dramatically behind the building. "They're, out there!" My interviews began with Miss Helena, whom I also asked to draw a map of the burial ground. "Thank you, I am grateful for your diligence." I secreted it in my jacket.

Suddenly, a hand grasped my right arm and short, pot-bellied Dr. Simons appeared. I winced at his tight compression and he let go. His skin was bumpy, face misshapen, his nose a blob beneath two small eyes lost in his sunken wrinkles. His mouth was like the deep cuts in my arm, a large gash in the lower half of his face. His grey moustache was a formless smudge on his lip. His clothes sagged as if rarely pressed. Jacket and tie had crumbs and stains upon them. Proportionately his hands were over-large, fingernails clean. He looked to be in his late fifties yet as energetic as an 18-year-old.

"I'm Dr. Herman Simons and you are new here orderly?"

"Adam Newton, sir," and put out my hand, which he grabbed and squeezed hard. I pulled away, "Really sir!"

"Forgive me, please. Let's begin your training in the Simons' Method then. I'll introduce you to our little atrium group. Our patients are like members of our family."

"I'm honoured, thank you."

A woman half-dressed and singing to her doll was wandering around the atrium. "Take her hand!"

"This is not ethical, sir."

"Ethicality!" He took me aside, spoke in an angry whisper. "Many of these people are here because they have syphilis; how is that ethical? What treatment do they deserve? But they can fulfil a purpose for society and redeem their lives with the kind of experimentation I have devised. Do you know in Austria they are curing it with malarial fever?"

He took her doll, stroked it. The patient screamed and gesticulated wildly. "My baby!"

He said. "Can't I hold your baby? I will be careful."

The patient said. "Don't drop her!" She grabbed her doll and ran away into the crowd.

"She must be missing her child." I said.

"You are quick, Newton, but she is insane."

"You're the doctor, sir."

Simons reached for my head and I stepped back from him. "Phrenology is the study of the bones of the head: just by placing my hands on your head I can determine intelligence, information about your character, whether or not you lacked a certain personality trait, and even criminality. It should be required at every school in the land!"

He went for the hand of a young woman whose hair was cut incredibly short, pink skin showing through. "Miss Sarah, give me your hand." She complied as if under hypnosis. "Pretty Miss Sarah, she is a little shy about her beauty." He placed his hands on her head. "She is of moderate intelligence, lacks faith in life, larcenous." Took his hands from her head and drew a butter knife from her pocket. "Miss Sarah, where are your manners, say 'Hello' to this very handsome gent." He pocketed the knife and twirled her around to face me.

Miss Sarah, her eyes on the floor, said very quietly. "Hello."

I took the hand Dr. Simons thrust upon me, half bowed. "I am pleased to make your acquaintance, Miss Sarah. Do you like it here?"

She spat on the floor then ran back to her seat. Arms wrapped tightly around her body she rocked back and forth and was swallowed up by the crowd. Dr. Simons laughed. "You see how shy she is, and completely unaware of her beauty. We try to remind them of the qualities they have forgotten." His diligence at greeting every patient in some way was laudable and time-consuming, my interviews waited for another day.

"In preparation for the job, I read your founder's tenets."

"You want us to go backward, son? No, the Simons' Method will reach results in much less time. You'd be surprised how many of these sick people are entrusted to us by their families. It is more the norm than the exception."

Dr. Simons pounced on a nurse; playfully put his arm around her. "Our Nurse Nancy oversees this area and also teaches at our School for Nurses. Nurse, this is Adam Newton, the new orderly. Isn't he handsome?" I tipped my bowler.

She looked uncomfortable, and gently pushed Simons away. "How do you do, Mr. Newton, and welcome to Hudson. I'm sure you have been hearing about all our brand-new equipment and Dr. Simons' ideas." She put out her hand, I shook it.

"Thank you, nurse. Please see to your patients." He waved perfunctorily to the general area. "Upstairs are the bedrooms, showers, and dressing rooms. The south wing houses our modern therapeutic treatments.

"Dr. Burckhardt over in Marin, Switzerland, has some views of his own. I've applied them in conditions deemed to be intractable. He asserts that disordered minds are but a reflection of disordered brains, and that the best way to cure a patient is to remove the offending sections. Here at Hudson we have the most modern surgical theatres of any like hospital. We recently treated a young sodomite who was incapable of self-vigilance. He was cured in our operating theatre by castration."

Aghast at what I had just heard. "I'd like to speak with him, is he here?" I looked around at the patients in the atrium.

"Unfortunately he expired following his successful surgery." He watched for my reaction. "The positive aspects of this research are carried through for the future, to help others." He smiled.

I noticed there were no patients near the south wing. I buttoned my coat and swirled my long scarf around my neck. The hill was covered with new snow, but the paths were clear. I turned back. "Sir, when I arrived this morning, there was a serious event at the entrance. Will that man get a chance to talk with someone about why and where he was headed?"

He grabbed my left arm and positioned me as if I were his confidant, lowered his voice. "We saved that patient's life, he wouldn't last an hour dressed like that, out in his slippers in this weather. They have no common sense!" His grin widened. "The insane don't know what they want or need. We doctors, have the years of study, like fathers to wayward children, we know better. If one is committed here, it is frequently for life." He let go my arm, thumped my back, and pushed me toward the doorway. "Good reflexes and good balance. Do you box?"

"Yes, but I quit it."

He felt the muscles of my left arm. I stepped away. "Stopping before it altered your face was prudent."

I shook his hand and thanked him for his time.

This conundrum was well-defended. "Tight as wax," my partner would say. The techniques applied here were repellent but acceptable practice in this field. The Simons brothers remain unanswered questions in this dark horror. Dr. Joey seemed a generalist, he preferred to be professionally involved in all aspects of this pile, from the obligations of the lowest orderly and hiring, to all the legal paperwork generated from within the superintendent's office. While his brother persevered with his specialized quest for a cure, he represented Hudson at Lunacy Commission meetings. One may wonder which Simons was actually running Hudson. Yet, how could I keep Miss Marcello safe?

  I walked out and lit a cigarette. Breathing in the cold air, I was frozen to my spot by the sight of a long line of women climbing up the hill to the shelter of the asylum. They were secured to each other by a long cable fastened to wide leather belts, the belts locked around the waists of fifty women. Guarded by brutish attendants: they screamed, cursed, prayed, sang, and their distorted faces showed just how far each woman's journey from sanity had led.

  These were the violent patients out for an airing while their ward was cleaned. But why were these women shackled like convicts? And they were filthy. How was that medically necessary? The wind had no answer, it picked up, blowing the snow into drifts. Groups of well-supervised male patients with shovels headed inside, holding onto their hats. Dr. Joey took charge of the shovels. Who answered for this? Neither Simons' brother, it seemed. Was there some other evil embodiment hidden here? Without facts this was merely conjecture. Speculation combined with the awful dread of the asylum would lead me to unwelcome diversions.

  In the cab ride to Meyer's, I shared some of my less worrisome thoughts with Marcello, grateful for my dinner with him and the Houdini brothers. In the tavern we discussed plans for the rescue. I apprised Marcello of the position of the communications box which held the asylum's telegraph and telephone equipment and pressed upon him the necessity to arrive armed. Houdini and Dash explained their marvellous burlesque program to us and our warm laugher carried me home through the cold night.

 Palm Sunday was my second salaried day in the asylum. While the patients were at Sunday service, I jogged through the cramped, dusty grey light into the atrium's bright open space to Nurse Nancy. She led me to a remote outside classroom, where we sat in wooden chairs near the fireplace. I had hoped this meeting would clear some of my suppositions.

 "Miss Anthony and I are working in concert to help release Miss Rita Marcello," I said.

 "Do you mean Mrs. Pinto?" I nodded. "Mr. Newton, I hope you can, she is in danger. She speaks up for herself, and that is never a good thing. At Hudson, doctors are the top of the hierarchy, patients down at the bottom." I lit a cigarette, leaned forward and encouraged her to continue.

 "Would you mind if I also smoked? Some suffragists do."

 I offered my case and lit her cigarette and enjoyed the uncommon pleasure of smoking with a lady. This was not a rough dock woman with her cuty pipe, whom I have also had occasion to share tobacco with. But an educated, intelligent young medical professional and teacher, a real lady. It was one of my most pleasantly unique American experiences.

 "Most of those who question the doctors wind up in our experimental rooms." She looked in my eyes. "They don't make it back from that."

"Do they go to another hospital? Is there anything you can do from the inside to help Mrs. Pinto?"

She whispered. "I don't know what happens to them. They just disappear and are purged from the medical records. I can make sure she gets the things that have been taken away from her, like meals."

"Are you saying she is being starved?"

"No, just kept hungry. But I see family members are bringing picnics, encourage them to continue. Don't get me wrong, Rita is a good patient. She questions a doctor's decision when she thinks it could be harmful, and they see that as rebellious. She is more intelligent than most of the doctors at Hudson and they don't acknowledge a woman's intelligence, so they see it as a problem."

"What about her safety, can you help with that?"

She looked at the door. "I have no authority over either Dr. Simons, or any of the doctors, on the wards, but I can help her."

"What would they do to her?"

"People like Rita are usually scheduled for frequent private sessions." She shook her head.

I waved her on to elaborate, leaned back in my chair, and closed my eyes.

"Some doctors enjoy keeping patients awake to their total power over them. They feel it's quite a challenge to whip their wayward children into shape. Their poor charges, women and men alike, need iron discipline." I was intently listening to her. I opened my eyes, and she was looking directly at me.

"I am not squeamish, pray continue." I closed my eyes, put my fingertips together.

"In their quest to break her down, they refuse her things, access to the showers, meals, her personal things. They have so little here, but all of it can be removed on a doctor's say-so: Blankets, clothing, outside access, the gardens, classes, safe wards. And then there are restraints, which some use as punishment. She can be thrown up to the violent ward at any time and they will do their dirty work."

I urged her on.

"What goes on in those private sessions? I don't know. They are cloistered and confidential. But a woman patient once told me she was raped. Though I'm not sure what she meant by that, vaginal, oral, anal, or did he just touch or kiss her? I wasn't the examining nurse, and women grow up so insulated. I have dressed men's caning wounds. Some believe the patients need to be purified or shocked awake. And I think some of the doctors enjoy it a little too much."

I opened my eyes. "Do you think there are sadists at Hudson Hospital, Nurse Nancy? Do you know who they are?"

"Yes. But finding them won't be easy."

"This will need more consideration on my part. The situation is very dark. But if you can keep Mrs. Pinto safe, I will do all I can for her release and to bring these doctors to justice." She nodded.

"How will you do that, Mr. Newton?" I lit another cigarette and offered her one.

"The Simons brothers are alone in their high towers. The other doctor's feelings are personally involved. They are as yet unknown to me. One of them will make a mistake. They have probably made many already. But now you and I are watching and we will catch them."

"You sound so sure."

"I have seen many like men go down." I released a swirling cloud of smoke above us. "Villainy will always be conquered by those whose hearts and minds are inclined to justice."

"Justice in a State Hospital for the Insane?"

"Justice is a right of citizenship."

"There is one doctor you may meet today, Dr. Edwards. He's a weekender, and usually here on Sundays." She pitched her cigarette into the fire and said with a shake of her head. "What will you do if justice fails you?"

"An escape has been planned and your assistance appreciated." I put out my fag.

"Yes I've heard." She smiled.

"So what can you do to keep her safe?" I lit us both another cigarette.

"I can get her out of restraints, out of the violent ward immediately. I'll talk with her after her sessions. Remove any restrictions placed on her." She put her hand to her throat, said in a quavering voice. "If they notice I'm doing this, they'll probably kill us both." She crushed out her cigarette.

"Kill! That is a serious charge."

"There are rumours that two bodies are buried in unmarked graves on the grounds."

"Is there any evidence, Nurse?"

"Nothing."

"I would be careful about repeating injurious rumours, Nurse Nancy. I am not asking you to put yourself in harm's way, but to help Mrs. Pinto when it is safe for you to do so. Please get a message to me if your lives are threatened or if you catch a doctor in an indiscretion." I wrote down my Vassar information. We walked out of the schoolroom and returned to the asylum building and the continuance of our work day.

I positioned myself to encounter Dr. Edwards as he entered the hospital. "I am Orderly Newton, sir, glad to meet you."

He blandly shook my hand. "Orderly, bring my first patient."

He was mousey, medium height and build, brown hair, and brown eyes. Pug nose, nails bitten to the quick, like Lestrade he wore greyish brown. His overall mien was one of invisibility. He was soft-spoken, genteel, with a pencil moustache lining his thin upper lip.

Edwards was to attend patients privately throughout the day. I escorted an exceptionally beautiful young man to Edwards' door. The patient's name was Will, and he spoke the Queen's English in a resonant baritone. When he came out he was clearly in pain and holding back tears.

"Will, what's wrong?"

"Nothing."

"I am new at Hudson and petitioning patients about their treatment by the staff. I want to weed out the bad apples. Can you help me?"

"I'm afraid of what they'll do to me."

"I can help you son. You must trust me. I am not under anyone's thumb here, but a free agent." I put my hand on his shoulder and he winced and pulled away.

"I have a smoking area behind the schoolroom, come out and we can talk."

He drew me a picture of pure sadism and I directed him to Nurse Nancy for the immediate attendance of his wound. Dr. Edwards' Gladstone bag was filled with scourges. The horrible devises that some believed would bring them to a holy state and one of the reasons I decried religion. His therapy was comprised of directing his patients to painfully scourge themselves, while he recited their sins. For the rest of the day, I ensured no patients entered his office. It seemed a summer complaint had infected the men's ward. I left a full report on Simons' desk. A trap set to spring.

Watson, it is a cruel world.

The innocent souls trapped inside that red brick fortress haunt me. This is the new way of the state; yet, I can see nothing but torment here. Both brothers, the Superintendent and his assistant, seem distasteful, yet I can find nothing to hang them on. Do I not have the expertise?

How does it help the unbalanced mind to be treated thus? How are doctors deluded into thinking this is an ameliorative environment? Once again we see society's foolish application of power and control against the powerless. But who, who is regimenting this? I have unmasked one villain, but he is no general.

I will see justice done!

Goodnight, dear Watson. The great Cicero I think had our partnership in mind when he wrote: "Amicitiae nostrae memoriam spero sempiternam fore:—I hope that the memory of our friendship will be everlasting."

As you know me to be, dear friend,
Very sincerely yours,
S. H.

CHAPTER 19
A RIVER OF FEAR

"I shuddered to think how completely the insane were in the power of their keepers, and how one could weep and plead for release, and all of no avail, if the keepers were so minded."–Nellie Bly. "Ten Days in a Mad-House."

My dear Watson,

We are at the beginning of the end. My undercover endeavour shows substantial audacious possibilities. A strong malevolence pervades this ziggurat, yet its villainous core has so far eluded me. More temerity is needed.

Thank you, Watson, for always being my rock bottom support, and I hope you do know just how much I need you, together we are formidable.

As you know me to be, dear friend,
Very sincerely yours,
S. H.

Monday proved to be my final day of employment as an orderly. At 8 a.m., Dr. Joey and I awaited Miss Marietta's arrival at the entrance. "Doctor, your brother is an interesting man. Constantly assessing the temperature of the world around him and seems to be up-to-date with new methods." I said.

"That's Herman to a 'T.'" He turned and walked away.

Miss Marietta arrived and was allowed into Hudson to visit with Miss Rita. Her package and the clothing within were searched and returned to her. I offered my arm and led her through the grey hallways to her sister in the atrium. She went in to change, returned, and revolved for Marietta's inspection. "What do you think?"

"Beautiful, you look like someone soon to be leaving this place." She shook her finger at her sister. "Now, don't laugh and please be your demure self. I'll wait for you here. Cara's *schiacciata* and Giuseppe's sweet sausage are our picnic today."

Orderly Newton played his part as her escort. "It's a big day for you Mrs. Pinto."

Acting her role she looked down at the floor. "Yes sir."

I conducted her to a windowless, white-walled doctor's office. Two doctors were heads together at the desk in the examination room. They did not introduce themselves, but I knew them. Dr. Feldman a small, thin, almost dainty gentleman, with immaculate hands and mild intelligence. Dr. Lacassio, handsome Roman features, tall, white maned, arrogant, he observed Miss Rita closely as she walked to her seat.

"We will be with you." Lacassio waved me to another chair by the door.

"Feldman, your first time? Don't worry, it's not our confession. Here's the Certificate of Lunacy, two copies. We sign here at the top and then again here at the bottom if we find her insane." They turned to her.

Miss Rita had disclosed to me that she would present an image of the perfect gentlewoman: unassuming, quiet, witless, unquestioning, helpful, graceful, agreeable, and the model patient.

Lacassio dictated the instructions. "Mrs. Pinto, we will ask you a series of questions. Some may seem strange, just answer as best you can, my dear." He lightly stroked her hair. "Now pay attention." He cupped her chin, and growled. "Because your dear life is in my hand."

She started.

"What is the day of the week?" He began walking slowly around her.

"Doctor it's Monday, the 19th of March."

"Where is this little love nest?"

"This is an examination room inside the Hudson River State Hospital, doctor."

"Can you spell backward the word 'kayak?'" Feldman nudged him and whispered in his ear. "Well, 'world' then."

"K-A-Y-A-K and D-L-R-O-W."

Lacassio placed his hand on Miss Rita's waist. "Not a Gibson Girl are we, you must have children, so much the better." I cleared my throat and he glared at me.

He moved in front of her. "Please repeat this saying: 'Is adultery sweeter than the same old thing at home?'"

"Is adultery sweeter than the same old thing at home?"

"Can you tell me what it means?"

"Like all proverbs, it can have different meanings. I think the most used is, 'Hell is not worth a moment's fancy."

Lacassio laughed, and kissed Miss Rita's hand. "You are of Italian descent, are you not Rita?"

"Yes, doctor, first-generation American. My parents were from Bari, Italy."

Lacassio smiled, nodded his approval, and continued. "Do you always wear glasses?"

"Yes, doctor."

"Would you take them off for me?" He dropped them on the floor and crushed them with his boot. Miss Rita gasped and then gained control.

"Do you have any other deformities?"

"No doctor."

"Please tell us the plot of your favourite book."

"I'd be happy to. The great detective, Sherlock Holmes, is hired by the King of Bohemia to recover a compromising photograph. Mr. Holmes dons many disguises as he attempts to trick Miss Irene Adler, the opera contralto, into showing him where it is. His masterfully created personas fool her, but she figures him out in the end and escapes with the photograph, beating Sherlock Holmes at his own game. It's 'A Scandal in Bohemia,' by Dr. John H. Watson."

Lacassio helped her out of her suit jacket, whispered in her ear. "What would I mean if I said I was feeling blue? Seeing red? Or was hot under the collar?"

"Feeling blue is sad, seeing red is anger. Hot under the collar is upset or angry."

"Or it could be arousal." Lacassio sneered.

I jumped up and from the back. "Doctor, decorum, please!" Lacassio stared at me for a moment. "Are you new here, orderly?"

"Yes doctor."

"Good, this will be your education. At a word from me, you will lose that new job!"

I nodded.

"Now Dr. Feldman and I will perform a physical examination, then you can go, Mrs. Pinto. But I can see you may need more time with me before I give my final decision." He licked his lips.

Feldman led her to the examination table and closed the curtains. "Mrs. Pinto, would you disrobe and step up onto the table for me?" He went through the short physical and wrote down his findings.

Lacassio yanked off his lab coat and jacket, pushed Feldman away, leaped onto the examination table and began to unbutton his trousers. "You know Mrs. Pinto it's rare to get another chance at this exam." I ran to her. "And you a married woman must feel it too."

I ripped the curtain open and one uppercut decked Lacassio, knocking him off the table.

Miss Rita fastened her skirt and blouse. "I believe this examination is over." She said. I retrieved her jacket from the chair and draped it round her shoulders. At the opened door she showed more of her immense courage. "Dr. Feldman, would you give me an idea of the test's outcome?"

"We will let you know." Feldman said.

I brought Miss Rita out. She nodded to me, and walked to her sister in the solarium. I then brought Nurse Nancy into the examination room. The curtains were open, and Lacassio was probing his chin. He pulled on his lab coat.

"You can sit, nurse, if you'd like." Feldman said. "Just one question for you: Do you think Mrs. Pinto can perform the activities of daily living, such as dressing, eating, and bathing?"

"Yes, Mrs. Pinto has no problem with daily living activities, as she has taken care of herself since she arrived here. And she has helped other residents."

"Thank you, nurse." As she left, Lacassio said. "Orderly, stay a moment."

He swiftly grabbed my jacket front, and slapped my face hard. "What you experienced is easily forgotten, make sure you do."

I tore his hand off me. "Mrs. Pinto is clearly not insane, doctor. If you care as much as you seem to, surely you can help her to go home to her loving family."

"When this hospital allows a lowly orderly to make a doctor's diagnosis, then I will listen to what you have to say. Your days are numbered, and your show of violence has consequences."

I walked out. Dr. Edwards hastened out of Simons' office, charged past me and into Lacassio's examination room. A moment passed and they re-emerged. Lacassio angrily approached me and shouted to the other attendants: "Come, gentlemen! This dangerous and violent man is in need of some restraint!" Edwards signalled to an orderly, who grabbed my wrists. A simple Baritsu escape move freed me, and I ran toward the front exit. Another orderly arrived with a straitjacket and I decked him with a hard left. Another attendant appeared. I tripped him, and threw him at the first one. Dr. Edwards plunged a needle into my thigh, and I swiftly moved away, using his fingers to pull it out.

"Newton, by this time tomorrow, your life will take a very different turn." Lacassio laughed and waved on more attendants.

A third grabbed me from behind, and I threw him over my shoulder, but the last two instantly thrust the jacket over my head and began to strap me into it. I used the as yet unattached arms as whips and beat them away from me. My escape was now clear and I sprinted for the entrance but the yellow pine floor had become a soft gelatinous caramel, and the last thing I remembered was hitting it.

―――

Groggily I climbed the ladder toward cognizance and heard menacing whispers: "Nice little show you put on! Almost made it, but my men stood the test. You think you can fool me? I'll teach you! How in hell did you get those slashes? Are you an addict, Newton? No matter, what are you but meat to be fired?"

I was awakened fully by someone yelling in the voice of Sherlock Holmes. I couldn't move. I opened my eyes to excruciatingly bright daylight, closed them again. Not a coffin then. I was on my back, lying face up on a mattress, painfully crammed into a tightfitting box. My eyes opened to slits. It was 12 inches high, 3 feet wide, and not long enough for me. There were slats on all sides and a slated top that locked to close me inside what I knew to be a Utica Crib. The crib was a restraint device for out of control or violent asylum patients. I could move my arms slightly but my knees were bent to fit into it, I could only see out through the bars in the direction I lay. A feeling as foreign as surprise, to me stood my hair on end. The only defence I had was the wondrous practice the Lhasa monks had taught me. Automatically I took a meditative breath, and let the fear pass. I took another.

The whitewashed room was familiar, I looked at my right hand and dark animal fur grew up my arm while long raptor claws projected from my fingers. Logic told me I must be drugged. Probably morphine mixed with something. That is fortunate for I have some tolerance for morphine. Again I attempted to get out but to no avail, I was held fast, it was spring-locked on the outside. I will be released and take it from there. I breathed again.

I heard far-off screams. Directly above this room were those who made their displeasure known. There were one hundred beds rammed up against each other: rolled up mattresses on hardwood planks and a pillow for each one, but no blankets or bedding. Windows filled two walls, but they were locked and barred with no curtains. There were two ways in and out, I knew, front and back stairs.

My brain was wrapped in cotton, I was intensely thirsty, my body screamed for release from this bondage, and a cigarette would be most welcome. I wondered how Houdini would approach this. Probably the addition of a small saw to the lock pick in his mouth and a studied practice of the lock. What did I remember about it? One was located by my feet and these spring locks could only be opened from the outside. Could I escape? Not enough room for a solid kick or to get my hand through. It was designed for the frenzy of the insane. Houdini's size would allow him to move around and he could probably pick the lock with his toes. The idea of that brought me to laughter.

Dr. Joey had related that inhabitants became calm and quiet after a time. Pure energy shot through my arms and legs. With all my strength my arms forced against the slats of my cage to no avail. I searched for a weak slat and kicked repeatedly with my knees. Could I escape? Without money, coat, or my boots, I'd have to find a cab before freezing to death. But all obstacles can be overcome. As I've asked innumerable terrified clients, "Trust in me, Holmes."

I took another breath and Will appeared. "My dear sir, are you all right?"

"Will, get me out of this coffin!" He quickly released the locks and threw wide the lid. I leapt out of the monstrous chamber, holding onto him for support. "Thank you, and do you know what they have planned for me?"

"If you're here, they will keep you drugged like a violent patient. I think that's for now. This is a tough place to wake up. Is there anyone I can contact for you, family, or friends?"

"Where is the lavatory? I'm going to need to lean on you to get there." I stood and stretched my legs, arms, and my back. "Oh, that is good!"

"I'll help you."

"Thank you." I washed my face and hands in the trough-like sink, and drank my fill of the ice cold water.

"How is your shoulder?"

"Thank you, the nurse took care of me."

"Did you suffer any repercussions from my report to Simons?"

"I will not walk through that door again. Simons is now my doctor."

"Now, what is my protocol? I am starving and a cigarette right now would be beneficial."

"In this ward, you are confined to this facility, except for meals down in the dining room." He looked at his watch. "Lunch is in half an hour. You are not allowed out and I would keep far away from doctors. If you do see them act drugged. Going outside will get you time in the south wing. As a violent patient, that's experimental surgery. But the orderlies' locker room is just down those stairs."

"You seem like a fine young man. Why are you here?"

"I'm homosexual."

"That's it?"

"I like women, too."

I shook my head. "But such generosity of spirit is not a reason to be in an asylum."

"It's better than castration. From what I can see, very few of the inmates belong here. There are children, too. Most are just dumped off by their families because like me they are different or they're poor. I try to help them as much as I can."

"That's most commendable. You're British, what are you doing here?"

"I was studying acting, which my family thinks is an abomination, so they sent me to Riverview Military Academy in town. And they sent me here. One good thing about that is when I leave here it's only a short train ride to Broadway. But the pills I take bloat my body like this, so how can I continue as an actor?" He sighed. "Do you want to stop for a smoke before lunch?"

I ignored my shaking legs as we walked down. "I know it's difficult in this place, Will, but, our dreams are what make us who we are. If I can, I will help you, you must not lose faith."

CHAPTER 20
MRS. PINTO VS THE LUNACY COMMISSION

> "The insane asylum on Blackwell's Island is a human rat-trap. It is easy to get in, but once there it is impossible to get out."–Nellie Bly. "Ten Days in a Mad-House."

This interlude was related by Samuel Morse, to me, via hand-delivered note to my rooms at Vassar College.

Rachel pounded on the observatory door. "Mr. Morse, Mr. Morse, open up!"

"Child, three taps is all it takes, not yelling my name out into the night." He observed that she was upset and in some urgency.

"Mr. Morse, I haven't seen my friend, Professor Sigerson for days! I know his plans are coming together and I don't know what's going on. I'm terrified I'll lose them both! Can I come in?"

"Come in, come in, child. Stay as long as you like, I was just sitting down to tea, and your presence is fortuitous. Have a jelly donut."

"I need to organize my thoughts and decide what to do. I don't know what to do. I hate not knowing what to do!" She accepted the donut and absentmindedly took a bite, the sweet scarlet jam dripped down her chin.

Morse poured them both a cup of tea and indicated the milk and honey. "Surely there are others involved in helping the professor." He handed her a napkin.

"My Uncle Oscar and Houdini are planning something. But I'm so afraid. The two people I care most about are in that horrible place." She stirred honey into her tea.

"Sometimes waiting, especially not knowing what's going on, is the worst thing, feels horrible. Something children go through a lot, yes?"

"Nobody tells me anything! I started this whole thing and got Professor Sigerson involved. You know how important he is. If anything happens to him, it'll be all my fault!" She began hyperventilating.

Morse patted her hand. "My dear, it may feel that way but it's not true. And he'd be the first to say so." She began to relax. He moved to the telescope, adjusted the height. "Unless you're a villain or a lawyer, most of what happens in life is no one's fault. Your actions are laudable, not lamentable, and even heroic, Miss Rachel."

Her breathing slowed to a fast normal. "Heroic, me?"

"You do know your professor is a hero?" She smiled. "He knows how to take care of himself in dire situations. He's been in worse places than Hudson. And he always lands on his feet. He's a master of defence, he finds cohorts who trust him completely because he is a gentleman of his word, and nothing frightens him. It's that mind of his. I'm fast but he lives almost in a different time from the rest of us. He sees how everything works together and looks at the world like a chess board."

"That's what terrifies me, they can destroy his mind! I just wanted him to take my aunt out of that place, but it's turned into something horribly treacherous and scary!"

"Actually, I have something to add to that rescue you are planning. I'll show you and you can teach your uncle how to cut through all the telecommunications wires at the asylum. Tell your uncle it takes but a few seconds."

"We can do that? It would be a helpful thing, wouldn't it? They couldn't call for the police. Thank you, please show me."

"It's just a matter of carefully clipping these wires." Morse pointed to a comprehensive sketch which he had made. The design is the same for all state buildings." He cackled. "I made it myself." Then he rummaged in a large box. "He can safely cut them with this." And he handed the child the tool and his instructions.

"Thank you. Tomorrow is my aunt's trial and she will either come home or the rescue plan will go into action. And this plan just might end in both of them taking a steamship across the ocean, and I may never see either of them again!"

He sighed. "My dear, surely helping the rescue in this way, gives you some happiness?" He pointed to her. "When you bestow this to your uncle, remember I don't exist!"

"Yes, sir"

Morse sent telegrams in the child's name to Oscar Marcello at Perry Street and at Abbott's Boarding House and sent a student off to my rooms in Main.

I travelled down the asylum's stairs. With each step I regained my strength and entered the locker room where Dr. Joey was lighting his pipe. He was not surprised to see me.

"You are finding your way, Newton." He said. "That was some fight! We'll be talking about it for some time." He smoked, sized me up. "My brother thinks we ought to enlist you in the real thing. What do you think?"

"If it gets me out of here, I wouldn't mind a little bare-knuckled workout, actually would enjoy it. What does your brother have in mind?" I said.

"Involving his cronies and a local kid coming up, George McFadden. Have you heard of him? Plus a lot of drinking and betting to raise funds. It should be a match."

"Tell your brother, I'll do it. But I want my freedom, win or lose."

"I'll let him know."

"Do you follow in his footsteps or are you your own man?"

"Herman has his methods and I have mine."

"What is your method?"

"More down to earth."

"And your brother's method?"

"He's testing so many apparatus' and in a rush to put his name on one. His is a high-stakes approach. So, I'd be careful, if I were you." He knocked out his pipe and left.

I checked the locker that held my coat and found it and my cigarettes. One step closer to escape. I lit one and picked the evening edition of the *Poughkeepsie Daily Eagle* newspaper from the bench. Its front page headline arrested my attention:

Susan B. Anthony Foiled at Trial

"At 9 a.m. this morning, inside the wood-panelled Dutchess County Courthouse, a drama was enacted at 10 Market Street. You will recall that in 1788, on this site after much discussion, our esteemed State of New York ratified the United States Constitution. The first case in Judge Danforth's courtroom this morning concerned a patient from the Hudson River State Hospital for the Insane. Judge Danforth has had a fair and honoured career in our beloved city.

Miss Susan B. Anthony spoke from the witness stand in support of the defendant. Miss Anthony is a leader in the New York–based National Woman Suffrage Association. She said. "I have known the defendant for many years. She is level headed, caring of her family, intelligent, honest and God-fearing. I find that many intelligent women have been locked up in asylums against their will. It is a travesty which ruins families and robs children of their mother. The defendant was put into the Hudson River State Hospital against her will by her cruel drunkard husband, and you have the chance today to right that wrong, Judge Danforth. I beseech you to do so."

Doctors Lacassio and Feldman represented the hospital. The judge ruled against the patient: "As this is a medical judgment, the court decrees that the defendant will return to the hospital for one month." Despite the attentions of Miss Anthony, Judge Danforth ruled to send the patient back to the asylum for further testing.

This was concordant with one of the hospital's most important duties: to keep our community safe from altercations committed by the insane. It seemed a fair and lenient ruling to this reporter.

I threw the paper to the floor. Marcello and Miss Anthony would arrive here at 8 a.m. tomorrow morning. I must alert Rita.

CHAPTER 21
THE SOLUTION

"But here was a woman taken without her own consent from the free world to an asylum and there given no chance to prove her sanity. Confined most probably for life behind asylum bars, without even being told . . . the why and wherefore. Compare this with a criminal, who is given every chance to prove his innocence. Who would not rather be a murderer and take the chance for life than be declared insane, without hope of escape?"–Nellie Bly. "Ten Days in a Mad-House."

My dear Watson,

I know every inch of this horrid monstrosity and its villainous doctors. And I long with every fibre of my being to fill Inspector Lestrade's growlers withal.

I have already given years of my life to the demise of one heinous crime organization. This one belongs to another.

Today is the rescue of one good soul to freedom and quite likely a few more. You know how gratifying that is, dear boy, worth everything.

As you know me to be, dear friend,
Very sincerely yours,
S. H.

Players in the game each relayed news of their part in it so I could present the story as cohesively as possible. It unfolds in sequence, yet shifts between six fronts.

In the harbour, overseen by the Poughkeepsie Ice Yacht Club, the National Challenge Pennant of America Race had been setting up since dawn. I knew my ward-mates watched on the asylum hilltop at the upper turret windows. Using cigarettes as currency, their lively wager progressed. The row of paper white sails stood in readiness. The signal was given, and they raced down the frozen Hudson toward Newburgh. I envisioned it all and surmised the winner, too.

———

Oscar Marcello and Miss Marietta readied for their part in the drama. He said. "Check your gun, and make sure it is safe in your pocket, be careful with that hair trigger." The cab had stopped near the entrance to the building to block their view. Miss Marietta in the cab took time to adjust her gloves and hat. Marcello had jumped out quickly, stepped to the side, pried open the box and cut the wires. The asylum was now isolated from the world. Marcello opened the cab door for his sister and they moved to the fortress. He addressed the security nurse. "Good morning, we have an 8 a.m. appointment with Dr. Simons."

———

On the Conservatory stage the Houdini Brothers were setting up for a performance. This elegant showplace was far from the asylum's front door. The greenhouse building was filled with warmth and comfortability. Today's event was a rare celebration in honour of the hospital's staff. The bar was open, and a buffet was laid out. Hudson's doctors and staff were enjoying this unique event. Houdini drew their attention and began. "Magic is the sole science not accepted by scientists—!"

———

Nurse Nancy in the atrium led a class on ladies' proper dress. Women joined her class, and minutes later walked to the outbuilding looking no longer like inmates. She passed around warm clothes where needed, checked their shoes and boots. A group of ten children passed on their way to the school room, and she smiled to Helena whose suffragist garb fit right in today.

Marcello and Miss Marietta were escorted to the superintendent's office by an orderly.

"Welcome to Hudson Hospital. I am Dr. Simons. And you are Oscar Marcello?" They shook hands.

"Doctor, this is my sister, Marietta." He nodded in greeting.

"We have come to take Rita for a family outing."

Simons called a nurse, dismissed Marcello: "Yes, yes, no problem. Please fill this out."

The nurse arrived, and spoke with Simons. Marcello handed back the signed papers. "I'm so sorry." Simons turned and threw the papers into the coal stove, spoke in a cat purr. "You'll have to reschedule your luncheon. There must be some mistake. Mrs. Pinto's doctor has scheduled her for electrotherapy. You must understand it is experimental, the latest therapeutic method. The preparation takes some time and afterward she will be indisposed for a few days, it can take a lot out of them. But entirely necessary, please schedule something for next week. Excuse me. I'm sure you can find your way out. You might take this chance to enjoy the grounds, our spring buds will be opening soon." He left with the nurse.

Houdini knew full well the ball was now in his court when Simons entered the Conservatory. He shook hands with the superintendent. "I am happy to meet you, sir." Will was sitting in the front row, acting drugged and heckling the performers. Houdini took him as a volunteer from the audience. Will hammed it up as an over-drugged patient, tilting, leaning, falling all over Houdini as the audience howled with joy at his superbly crafted slapstick. He finally lost his balance and took a pratfall into the "Metamorphosis" trunk. Houdini and Dash locked the trunk, and turned it around. They opened it and pointed the trunk toward the audience. All they saw was an empty trunk!

With great misdirection, Houdini said: "Where did he go? A man can't fade into the air like smoke? Maybe he's sitting next to you?" He pointed to Simons. "Will someone please check to see if he's fallen on the floor?" There were waves of laughter from the audience as they tried to locate Will.

Marcello yelled, "To the south wing! Marietta, grab those keys and run!" As they plummeted down the stairs the screaming increased. They found me in an isolation room.

"My liberator!" I hugged him and quickly attired. We found Miss Rita in an electrics room. She was being hooked up to the machinery, a rubber gag in her mouth, terror in her eyes. I secured my pistol from Miss Marietta, and Marcello and I forcefully broke down the door.

Suffragists simultaneously waving signs and chanting loudly poured through the asylum gates, "Votes for Women!" Miss Anthony led the chant as the gold in their sashes flashed in the morning sunlight. Their righteous energy cut through the darkness around them like fiery Amazon swords. Nurse Nancy guided the escapees into their jackets and sashes. The chanting increased as newly freed voices joined in.

Meanwhile, in the south wing, I roared, "Halt this abomination immediately! Stand away from Mrs. Pinto at once! That's right, now leave!" Her attendants ran out. Miss Marietta released her sister and helped her dress in the warm clothes she had brought with her.

In the observation hallway, shrieks were heard from other rooms. I raised my pistol and shot into the concrete ceiling. The noise accomplished its task beautifully and the attendants fled.

I grabbed Miss Marietta around her waist and kissed her. "Thank you for your courage."

"My pleasure," She squeezed my hand. "Danger is certainly an attractant."

I witnessed the excitement in her eyes and sighed. "There is more ahead!" Miss Rita ran to me and hugged, "Miss Rita, come, our carriage awaits."

The patients released, we formed an unusual corps as we made for the stairs. Miss Marietta wrapped her sister in her coat. Dr. Joey proved his worth as he appeared with the lift, welcomed in the rescued patients and encouraged them to join the march.

I led my contingent to the front door. "We withdraw this way. If we encounter Simons, leave him to me and escape with Miss Anthony's suffragists."

The Conservatory search was in progress. Houdini said. "I have studied the methods of Sherlock Holmes." And he produced an overlarge glass, donned a deerstalker hat and leapt into the audience, leading the search away from the stage. "He will be found!" Dr. Joey walked in and took a position behind the bar. He topped off drinks and had his bartenders hand around new libations. With these diversions, Dash led Will out of the building in the "Metamorphosis" trunk. He donned the clothing and found the funds I'd left for him. He then followed a trail Dr. Joey had blazed up through the woods to liberty.

Houdini pointed his glass. "By Jove, there he is in back!" Dr. Joey stood up doing his best imitation of Will, bowed and waved to everyone. Audience members laughed and patted him on the back. Houdini drew their attention to the stage, once more, to pose his final question. There were no serious takers. Houdini bowed and the asylum staff exploded in applause and cheers and he disappeared in a puff of smoke. It was at this time that the staff lost all ability to respond as their drinks had been spiked with morphine. Dr. Simons' orders became whispers. All they heard was the Houdini Brother's four-wheeler as the horses galloped past the Conservatory and headed for the train station.

The Marcello's and I ran out the asylum door, I draped my coat around Miss Marietta's shoulders and shouted for joy. "What-hey!" Houdini's escaping cab had flown by us and I leaped into our carriage, banged on the roof, "Let's go!" The driver flicked the horses to a trot. The sky was such a pure deep blue you knew the infinite stars were waiting beyond and the cold air filled my lungs with freedom.

Miss Rita looked into my eyes. "Thank you, professor."

"We both have more to accomplish before the day is out, Miss Marcello. How far south can you steer an iceboat?"

She smiled at me. "Below the race course certainly."

"Excellent, are you dressed for it?" I turned and witnessed Miss Anthony leading her suffragists towards the gate.

Miss Marietta said. "No she isn't. Keep the coat; take my jacket, gloves and hat, Rita." Such a singular woman!

Near the gate, Miss Anthony waved us on our way. Our cab swept through the entrance just in time to gallop off to the river. The marchers began their trek out of the paralyzed asylum toward Market Street. At the bottom of the hill I recognized one of the south wing attendants. He had jumped into a hansom aimed toward Mill Street. This brought the possibility of police involvement.

———

Near the Asylum gate, Miss Anthony led her marchers like a crack squadron down the hill to North Road and on to Washington Street. They chanted, "Equality for Women!" At Market Street she divided the march and led the escapees further on to Friends Meetinghouse at the corner of Montgomery and Carroll Streets. Townspeople lined the sidewalks of Main Street and Market Street in anticipation of the parade. In front of the opera house, the larger portion of the suffragist march collided with the Phoenix Hose Company's 50th anniversary parade on the way to its celebration. The women chanted "Votes for Women!" and the band played disconsolate pieces of a Sousa March as the parade and march entwined. Poughkeepsie's Finest arrived and were enveloped in chaos. But, Inspector MacKinnon and his crew had taken a different road and were now close upon us.

———

I donned Marcello's coat, cap and gloves as Miss Rita and I fled the cab and slipped away to the frozen river. The fast sled team I had ordered was nowhere in sight! As Marcello urged their cabbie onward much of the inspector's police force followed them in the runaway carriage.

The Ice Yacht Challenge was past, and the skippers celebrated at Meyer's. Yet our race had just begun. Miss Rita and I commandeered the *Glacier*. We readied the yacht, her sails filled with the swift wind that urgently shot us downriver. Inspector MacKinnon roused boat drivers who then followed us in ice yachts. It was a race against time and skill. Below Newburgh, the ice became choppy, but if you knew her currents the yacht held. We were surrounded by the glorious blue green Appalachian Mountains. And the ice was fast. The group of white butterflies quickly caught up as their skippers rode the wind's tail to their advantage. So close their legal threatening could be heard above the wind.

Then Miss Rita captained our craft and competently read the river's course through the dangerous ice. They were still gaining and the race was now life and death, when suddenly from within the posse, a boat advanced to the front. Paulo and the child moved ahead of us all, she unfurled black and yellow, then red and white four quarter flags to convey: "Stop! Danger Ahead!" Miss Rita and I passed them as they perilously 180-degreed to stop above Tarrytown, and bravely faced down the squad of racing yachts and MacKinnon. One after another, the boats turned with them and stopped. Voices echoed through the yachts. "It's the Commodore!"

"Stop, this race ends here!" shouted Commodore Marcello. "You have gone as far south as you can safely go. I'll race you back to Meyer's for ale!" Paulo and the child led them back up river where Reilly was waiting with Vassar Ale for all. When the yachters recounted the tale of their race they were welcomed as heroes as no one had ever sailed a Hudson River Ice Yacht so far or so fast.

Significantly inaccessible, Miss Rita and I hooted and hollered our escape and climbed ashore at the village of Irvington-on-Hudson.

We were fortunate as the southbound Hudson River train pulled in as we raced to the station and into the first car.

During our trip south to New York, Miss Rita unfolded a monstrous horror. "Simons unlocked the door, kissed my hand and led me to the electrics room."

"This was this morning?"

"No, last night, he had me locked in a padded cell all yesterday. He said. 'Come my dear, would you like some tea? I am sorry to say that you are in need of some punishment."

I took her hands. "Punishment, quickly, tell me all!"

"I was to participate in his punition of Mr. Battaglia. 'Your gracious help is needed.' He used no rubber mat, no rubber gag for his mouth! He had moved all the batteries from the other electrics room to this one, so there were six attached to him and a cable that reached out the door. He asked the patient to manacle his own ankles to the table. Simons' shackled one wrist. He calmly attached the electrodes to metal plates on his head and then wet him down. Having been in one of those rooms, I am sure he had the batteries set to the highest level. He said, 'This young man is here because he is an abomination in the eyes of God. Please undress, Mrs. Pinto and take his hand gently to your breast. That's right. Now, Daniel?' The poor man was crying."

"What do you think, Mrs. Pinto?" Simons automatically shackled Mr. Battaglia's wrist.

"I think you should release him!" I said, and quickly dressed.

"No, no! This is no experiment, Mrs. Pinto!"

"It was horrible, so horrible!" Rita began to wail and sob, shake and cry.

I knew I had seconds before she lost control, and minutes before I retraced our race upriver. "Rita!" I slapped my hands in front of her face! "You must tell me the whole story, now. Look at me!" I turned her face to mine. "What do you know about this man, what does he look like? Time is running out." I said as I gauged our speed and distance and put my arm around her.

The brave woman began again. "He's Daniel Battaglia, about twenty-four, from Catskill, short, thin, light brown hair, no facial hair, and hazel eyes. He was at my birthday party, remember? Simons strapped him to the table and switched on the batteries." She sobbed.

"The rubber padding and mouthpiece are to prevent electrocution and wet down to improve conductivity?"

"Yes and to raise his level of fear, and mine"

She looked at me. "Simons' sweaty hand grabbed me and led me out to the hall, positioned me in front of the observation window. He checked my pulse! 'Rest yourself, my dear.' He closed the door and locked it. I flew at him to stop this insanity, but he restrained me in a straitjacket, and forced me to sit facing the observation window. Then he checked the levels and all at once he turned on the batteries. *'Heaven and I wept.'* It was hideous. Instantly Mr. Battaglia's body arched as far as possible in those restraints. He screamed once and then nothing, silence, a metallic smoke was all!"

"Are you sure Battaglia is dead?"

"Oh, *Madonna mea*, he burned from the inside out, professor! The flesh of his face where the electric plates were attached was burnt down to his skull, and the skin looked like charcoal around it, so hideous. Simons watched it and took extensive notes, and then collapsed. I ran up the stairs, out of the south wing and right into Will.

He released me from the jacket and wrapped me in a coat then steered me to the garden where I fell sobbing into his arms."

She leaned into me and I held her tightly until we arrived at the depot. "Thank you for your remarkable story. I will do my best to bring Simons to justice. But, Miss Marcello, I cannot accompany you, and must immediately retrace our steps." I took her hand and quickly led her through Grand Central Depot to the hansom stand where she climbed into a cab. Her last gift to me was a clarification. "Dr. Joey's name is actually Josiah Simons."

I thanked her, and asked for one more favour. "Miss Rita when you arrive please use Mrs. Stanton's telephone to immediately call Dr. Josiah at Hudson. Tell him who I am and instruct him to lock up the south wing and await my arrival. And let no one in, especially his brother! Do you have that?"

"Yes, professor and good luck."

I paid and ordered the cabby to transport her to West 62nd Street and sprinted for the northern express train to Poughkeepsie. The sun had already set as I hailed a cab up to the asylum.

Dr. Joey met me at the entrance. "Thank you for staying so late." I said. "Miss Rita informed me your true name is Josiah?"

"Another of my brother's little jokes, he had the staff call me the name he used in childhood. He never acknowledged me as a professional even though I was as involved as he was in the administration of Hudson. And yours is Sigerson? Professor, are you studying Hudson Asylum for an article, like that reporter for the *New York World?*"

"No. Might you find me a tape measure, a magnifying glass and at least ten envelopes? But stay out of your brother's office."

We plunged to the south wing where I searched for proof. One of the electrotherapy rooms certainly presented evidence that a small, contained explosion had occurred. Before Josiah could unlock the door, Simons appeared and charged at me yelling. "Joey, get me a straitjacket!"

"I am Keevan Sigerson, sir!" I said. He jolted and turned toward me. Enough time for me to pull his coat over his head. Dr. Josiah and I threw him in an isolation room for safekeeping.

I surveyed Dr. Josiah. "Murder is not something I can clean up, professor. My brother's stepped beyond my help this time."

I thumped his back. "Good man!" I threw off each layer of my outer clothing. Pulled out a recent New York acquisition, a Folding Pocket Kodak and released the shutter to photograph the condition of the room. Climbed onto the table in the dead man's position and laughed. "Ha! Doctor, what do you see on the ceiling?"

"My God that looks like false teeth!"

"The lower set, if I'm not mistaken!"

"Doctor, I believe his gag failed." I leapt to my feet, stood one legged on the table, and plucked the appliance from the ceiling. "Please put this in an envelope." I hopped to the floor and walked backwards on the balls of my feet, my hands in my waistcoat pockets, my body bent, in my usual way I searched for footprints. The shiny tile accommodated me. "Three sets of footprints, doctor, one ending at the table, and one running tiptoe to the door. So these are Simons' prints and they perfectly corroborate Miss Marcello's story." I stood a lamp at floor level and recorded this evidence with my camera, and then picked up three burnt and disfigured metal plates. "There is a fourth, doctor." I lay down on the floor and swept my hand beneath the cabinets. Held the fourth plate up above the table for the doctor to see, and he put them in an envelope. The electrodes also displayed considerable damage and I passed them to Dr. Josiah.

"Professor, do you know anything about the sabotaging of our phone and telegraph today?"

"Someone cut the wires? What a fortuitous circumstance."

"Luckily when the staff awoke from their morphia slumber in the conservatory our handyman was among them. He reconnected the wires with ease and I called the police."

Simons was pounding on the door. "I am Dr. Herman Simons! This is my hospital, I make the rules! I'll get you Sigerson! If it takes the rest of my life, I'll get you!" Dr. Josiah looked worried.

I waved it away. "It's just the old sweet song." I said. "Josiah that is no longer your brother, his monstrous crime has indeed moved him far beyond your love. Think to the future, doctor!"

I checked for fingerprints and found a print on the doorknob and a matching one on one of the batteries. As Dr. Josiah watched, I extracted Simons' fingerprints. "This is my own method; it is quicker and more advanced than the constabulary. Though they are not admissible as evidence, some of the more forward thinking members of the force and the bar may be influenced nonetheless."

"Sigerson, why you would create a better way to use fingerprints in a police investigation is beyond me." said Dr. Josiah.

"Exactly what your police force is going to say, and here they come." I took from my inner pocket a folded piece of paper. "This is Miss Helena's map showing where to find Mr. Battaglia's body. His face and head are badly burned. Please retain the law officers at the scene of the crime for the next half hour and leave me to examine your brother's office. Before they come through like a herd of buffalo, and wallow all over it. And I believe from their point of view, I am an escaped lunatic; do not give me away." I laughed like an inmate as I sprinted up the steps.

The police arrived via the lift, and with Dr. Josiah Simons at the helm took possession of the corpse, and the murderer.

CHAPTER 22
A BREAK IN THE CHAIN

"Violence does, in truth, recoil upon the violent, and the schemer falls into the pit which he digs for another."–Dr. John H. Watson. "The Adventure of the Speckled Band."

To involve the reader in all that occurred in the conclusion of this case would be to jabber on about trifles that could matter only to me. The idea of my involvement or any steps I may have or may not have taken toward a certain outcome would shortly fade away.

My dear Watson,
This is the culmination of one of the darkest cases I have ever investigated. Simons in his way is as loathsome as Moriarty himself. I cheerfully await our London reunion and the closing of Moriarty's case with our capture of his diabolical hunter for good and all.
Spring I know is waiting with the green life sprouting in our corner of England, and promises many new beginnings. The Marcello family will be missed. They saved me from myself and didn't even know it, or me. The fame of my alias is difficult to live with, yet also proved beneficial at times. To be picked out of a crowd is unsettling, and I eagerly anticipate London's anonymity.
As my biographer, you will presumably retell these adventures with more depth and breadth than I can possibly accomplish. Undoubtedly in a future Strand article the world will recognize your silver penning of a sensational finale while I could only offer the links in the chain of my reasoning.
Watson, in less than a fortnight, I will breathe the tobacco and gunpowder aroma of No. 221B, Baker Street, sleep in my own bed, and fill my tired eyes with your wry smile while endeavouring to

answer all those questions you have as fully as I can. Then what I will need is a good disturbing case to solve and you by my side. Let's hope London's criminal element will accommodate us.

As you know me to be, dear Watson,
Very sincerely yours,
S. H.

Late the following day, as evening darkened into night and the river fog facilitated clandestine meetings. Dr. Josiah Simons and I met at Morris Henry's office on Market Street.

"Welcome, gentlemen." He said. "I am at your service. It is my understanding that you want me to arbitrate this meeting?" He held out his hand to the doctor and then to me.

"Thank you for coming, doctor. Please forgive me gentlemen for upsetting your weekend like this." Mr. Henry waved us to chairs around his desk.

"If I may, Mr. Henry, your role here is as a confidential and professional witness. We will need to draw up legal documents and send them off tonight." He nodded to me.

I turned and looked into Josiah's eyes; put my hand on his shoulder. "Now, doctor, your brother has been unmasked and arrested for murder. As you know I have enough evidence to convict him. New York State will appoint someone in his place unless you act. What will you do?"

He said, with a half-smile. "I will, of course, assume the full superintendence of the hospital for the rest of my brother's term." Henry drew up the paperwork and a resume, which would be hand-carried immediately to the New York State Lunacy Commission in Albany.

"Congratulations, Dr. Simons." Mr. Henry and I stood and shook his hand.

He grinned at us. "Thank you, I will not abandon my charges, I hope to liberate them." His face turned serious. "But I don't believe in this approach to the mentally ill. Asylums are not hospitals but prisons. The inmates treated like criminals. And worse, the 'Bath of Surprise,' sedation drugs, 'electrotherapy', and psycho surgery, for example, are dangerous experiments created out of the frustration to find a simple cure for a complex problem. The hospital gets away with it because families don't know what to do with a mentally ill relative. It's too easy to be committed by a narrow-minded family member to the care of authorities who don't know how to cure this illness. The people committed into the care of these doctors have little chance of returning to their lives.

"Keeping people locked away from life as therapy is unconscionable ignorance. We have forgotten that life is sacred and people are our highest asset. I've watched patients awaken in our garden and it's not the work, it's the act of creation that lifts them from their turmoil."

"I will make the changes I can, but in a few years, a new superintendent, a new commission, will put their mark on it. I am one man who can make life better for those in my care today, but in the scheme of things, I am only one."

I patted him on the back. "It is your time, doctor." We lit cigars to celebrate.

"Now, gentlemen, please take a seat. There is another reason for calling this meeting: I will not be here for the trial of Herman Simons. The culmination of three years' work calls me back immediately to London. But you may take my statement of the facts of this case. I will leave my evidence for you to present to the court. Will you do that, Mr. Henry?" He nodded. "Please send your bill to my London address." With a smile, I handed him my Baker Street card.

"Last night, doctor, you asked me if I was Sigerson and I nodded. He has been a faithful alias to me through many adventures. But gentlemen it is time to put my mask aside. I am Sherlock Holmes." I bowed.

Henry smiled, stopped writing, rose and shook my hand. "I am very pleased to meet you, Mr. Holmes!"

Dr. Josiah Simons jumped up, thumped my back and pumped my hand throughout: "What? No wonder! No wonder. Thank you, Mr. Holmes, if not for you my brother would still be hurting innocent people."

"I doubt there will be a problem accepting a statement from Sherlock Holmes." Mr. Henry said.

"There may be some difficulty explaining that I am alive. My partner's prevalent penning of my supposed demise. How rapidly will this come to trial?"

"Two weeks, maybe more. Mr. Holmes, the court is used to the infallibility of my witnessing. Your testimony and evidence will carry the court."

"But you must hold back my statement and keep my identity secret for another week. While I steamship back to London. You can accept that statement now and I will telegraph when it can be revealed. My brother in London and a criminal I intend to put behind bars on my return are the only other persons who know I am alive. To everyone else I am Sigerson. It is of absolute importance that I meet with my partner, Dr. Watson, before the Poughkeepsie Police Force or the New York State Lunacy Commission contact him to verify my existence. Presently, I am in danger from assassins. Three years ago I demolished a European crime syndicate whose henchmen are still after me. Your town has provided me with a much needed safe haven. With my return to London, the final link in the chain will be forged and I will be free to assume my practice again.

"Rendell & Tweedy Photographers have the film I exposed at the asylum. They assured me the 8" by 10" prints of the negatives will be ready in one week's time. Thank you for your help, Mr. Henry. Shall we?" After I presented my testimony and was absolutely certain that the significance of the clues I had uncovered were understood in detail, I turned to Dr. Josiah Simons. "Have you heard of Eastern meditation? It's a simple practice I learned in Tibet that brought a centring and solace to my life. It is easily taught, and you could instruct your charges. In the East they believe that meditation is the solution to life's problems."

He took to it like a man who was accustomed to contemplating the growing flowers in his garden and we sat in meditation pose for twenty minutes. I left Josiah meditating, while I cabbed up the hill to Vassar humming the violin part to Beethoven's Fifth.

CHAPTER 23
A DANGEROUS RETROSPECTION

"Every truth we see is ours to give the world, not to keep for ourselves alone."–Elizabeth Cady Stanton. "The Solitude of Self."

My dear Watson,

You could already be a doting father, and I hope providence has gifted you this way. It would suit you, dear friend. I believe I have sufficiently kept my feelings apart, but it is unbearable to consider leaving the child tomorrow. I imagine I feel a little of what a proud parent does for his intelligent child: it has expanded me, taken me places I didn't know existed and quite against my will. But isn't that the way with children?

Much violin therapy will be needed back in our rooms at Baker Street. Your companionship will be of considerable benefit.

This will also be my last chance to speak with Miss Marcello and Mrs. Stanton. You may chuckle at this, Watson, but there are spectacularly intelligent women who will take on the world together. I now have eyes to recognize them.

As you have done many times in similar situations, the child attempted to engage me for the trip. There are times when my focus is inward and away from any interaction. I remember sharing this with you as one of the bad habits new roommates should know about on the day we met, old man. For some reason I will never understand, this causes distress in those with whom I associate. In her case it is needless worry, for my heart has already been charmed.

As you know me to be, dear fellow,
Very sincerely yours,
S. H.

The next morning I awoke to the front-page newspaper banner: "Asylum Doctor Henry Simons Arrested for Murder." My bags packed, I left for breakfast.

My view of women was changed by Irene Adler, not because she outwitted me, but that she did it with style, grace, a face a man might die for, and the intelligence I would use in her situation. She beat me yet as my equal, possibly more than my equal. Set apart from the commonplace nature that women emulated today, she opened my eyes to something new, something I couldn't dismiss. And I fell as only I could. But here she also beat me. In one hour I loved completely and lost hopelessly, unbeknownst to her, as I witnessed her marriage at St. Monica's. All kept like the petals of a flower closed in the pages of the token I wear always. I wouldn't need to wear anything of Moriarty's to remind me of all the times that professor had outsmarted me. No, Irene's token was a remembrance of when love touched me.

And now I knew there were others who lived outside the strictures imposed on women by society and I broadened to include them in my world. I encouraged my Vassar College students in that direction. Witnessing young minds awaken was one of the great gifts my association with Vassar had given me and I was forever grateful for this endowment.

The day I left, President Taylor found me in the midst of one of these conversations in the Rose Parlour. Taylor poured a cup of tea and pulled a chair up to the discussion. "Please continue." He said. And the intellectual argument progressed. My student youthfully defended her point while I argued its consequences. When she departed for her next class, Taylor said. "You're a lightning rod, Sigerson, my students have caught fire. Know that you are always welcome at Vassar. We will be creating an archaeology department, stay and help me build it."

I was deeply touched. "It is difficult to pull myself away from Vassar. Possibly this is my future, but for the present, I have much to complete in London. Giving me this chance to share what I've learned from my journeys has brought me incomparable joy. To watch students begin to see how they could move in the world as men do is unique for me, yet also exquisite. Everyone here is a pioneer. The light of this college shines brightly for the world to see its useless folly. Your offer is a most generous one but I must decline. Yet, I will keep in touch." We stood and shook hands. Taylor gave me a package. It looked like my cleaning, so I smiled and patted him on the back.

I went to my suite and collected my new violin and bags. Inside the package were the robes of a doctor of philosophy with Vassar's colours on the hood and a diploma: "Vassar College. Mr. Keevan Sigerson, Doctor of Archaeology." My face flushed and the feelings surprised me. I dabbed my eyes and lit a cigarette. Taylor was using all his ammunition. I dressed in my perfectly tailored new robes, and left the faculty apartments. Marie and Anne took my luggage. Students and fellow professors lined the halls of Vassar's second floor, all applauding as my students sang: "For he's a jolly good fellow and so say all of us!" I shook hands with the professors, Taylor, and my students, and left magnificent Main for the last time.

My cab whisked me through Mr. Gatehouse's archway to the Marcello's home to collect the child. She was dressed in a female version of a sailor's suit. I jumped from the cab to hug Miss Marietta farewell. "Engage your dreams, Miss Marcello. Good luck in your California adventure."

"If you change your mind about smoky old London, you know where to find me, Professor Sigerson."

"I will not leave London again. Yet, I would welcome a chance to change your mind about my city, if you would allow." I gently wiped her tears and kissed her hand. *"Au revoir!"*

The child and I raced to the Poughkeepsie train station, and hopped on the Hudson River Railroad to meet Oscar in Manhattan. And I had the perfect disguise.

The girl said. "How terrific you look in your new robes, Professor Sigerson, now you can be one of my professors!"

"Child, the future is yet to be written."

She recited her favourite aspects of Grand Central Depot: "It opened in 1871, and the building covered twenty-one acres in the city. Soon its great arches will lead us into the largest indoor space in all America! It's 100 feet high, and 200 feet wide." She held her arms out. "And more than 600 feet long."

And I lapsed into meditation.

Following the river south, after firing five unanswered questions at me, the child accepted my adult necessity for occasional solitude. As we drew nearer to the city, her excitement became uncontrollable. I lit a cigarette, and invited her in with a wave of my hand.

"Professor, what are your plans? Do we see Uncle Oscar first or Mrs. Stanton? When is your boat? Can I come on board? I'd love to see this floating city."

"Child, I have some dangerous tasks ahead of me. In my European research into the underworld I discovered that each country's criminals have close connections in other lands. By now there will be watchers posted in the Depot or on the docks." I took out my revolver, checked it, and put it in my pocket. "First, you must understand that we may encounter villainous men in the city until my ship departs."

"What! What can I do?"

"Stay close to me, follow my orders without question and we will be all right, your hierarchical apparel is appropriate to our situation. We will meet with your uncle first and last as he will rendezvous with us via cab at Mrs. Stanton's home."

We arrived in New York through the depot's labyrinthine rails, screeching and flashing over the seemingly infinite amount of points. "Remember, we keep to the shadows."

"This is terrifying. I will do my best to keep you safe." She said.

Her arms crossed, her face determined. I acknowledged her earnest expressions of love, worry, her protectiveness, by putting my hand on her shoulder. "Child, this is my assignment. The best way for you to protect both of us is to implicitly follow my directions."

We disembarked at the platform, emerging at the depot.

Scouring the mammoth structure, I spotted a possible watcher moving away from us toward the Forty-Second Street exit. I now set her between me and the information kiosk. She followed my line of sight, observed my sudden change, and then wrapped herself around me.

I moved her quickly to the other side of the booth. "It is not a childish thing to stand between danger and a loved one, no matter how old one is. It is foolish, yet also courageous. Thank you, child, please inform me immediately if you observe anything suspicious. But as I am more suited, I will take the protector role today."

"You mean like that lookout? Aye, Aye, sir!" She saluted me then surveyed the whole of the enormous depot. I now had directions to the freight tracks where we stayed behind luggage carts all the way.

Marcello was surprised to find us so deep within the recesses of the depot. I immediately signalled to him to keep close and we three moved to safety. "The freight section is a part of the station few people ever see." He pointed the way. "Our car is on the next track." He took the child by the hand. "New York is a twenty-four-hour town. You can always find something open, and in those late hours, filled with the beauties of the stage."

"The most beautiful and gracious of women." I said, as I tapped the gold sovereign on my watch chain.

Marcello looked at me. "You are a man of mystery, Sigerson. So what is the story of that coin?"

"Something I lost a long time ago. Yet, the notion never leaves me, like a delicate, radiant, and oft reprised refrain."

"Oh, man, if she's alive, go get her. If she's not, find another."

"You are a wise young man, Marcello, and I am going to miss you." I clapped him on the back.

When we arrived at the transcontinental freight track, the sculptors had painted on the wooden car, in grand and glorious artist's lettering: "SAN FRANSICO WORLD'S FAIR OR BUST!"

"Sigerson, there's a piece we are about to load. It's my final New York submission. I'd like you to see it. Rachel, come over here for a better view." He pointed the way. "The pieces we are contributing all represent human sensibility as interpreted through the eyes and hands of the Impressionist School. I took some liberties with this one, however." He led me to the other side of the car. "I call it *'Virtuoso.'*"

It was a sculpture of me with my violin, yet fifteen feet high. It was playing as I did for him, eyes closed, head back, long hair loose and wild as if in a tempest. This virtuoso was bare-chested and muscled. Marcello had modelled my scarred arm and the bleeding knife cut across the chest, plus the needle marks on my left arm. I was caught completely unawares, and as tears formed in my eyes, he grabbed me in an Italian bear hug. "I'm sorry, Sigerson. Rachel will tell you that I never can resist a touch of the dramatic."

Pink-cheeked, I said. "Marcello, I've never been so honoured. Yet I don't think my mane has ever been so uncivilized."

"Creative license!"

"Something I heartily support." We laughed. "Please send me a photograph."

"I saved you the original drawing, Sigerson. It should do until the fair." He signed it.

"I will frame it, thank you, Marcello."

He looked in my eyes. "Sigerson, remember that day you ran up to my studio and I hastily covered up a sculpture? You caught me in the lie, I know you did. I wanted you to see it completed."

The child took my hand, gave me her handkerchief.

We left Marcello to his work and hired a cab from the stand, and completed our journey to West 62nd Street. Wrapped up in warm rugs, we travelled across town by way of 59th Street with snow-covered Central Park on one side and the city on the other.

Miss Marcello greeted us at the door and twirled the child around in her joy. Then she hugged me. "I'm so glad to see you. Do you have to leave so soon?" She brought us into Mrs. Stanton's greenhouse office overlooking the park. This small white haired, grandmotherly woman, with a brilliant light in her eyes that betrayed all she had accomplished, sat at her desk in a comfortable chair. She was composing her radical magnum opus, "The Women's Bible."

"Miss Rachel, please find seats and join me. Isn't this view magnificent? I never get tired of it. Professor sending Rita to me unescorted was most ungentlemanly."

"It was paramount, as the evidence of murder fades fast."

Mrs. Stanton looked up at me with a raised eyebrow.

I kissed her hand. "I am sorry yet I do have a steamship to catch." I turned to her. "Miss Marcello, I have the happy task of imparting the news that your release has been approved from Hudson Asylum. You're free, and may return home today with your niece and you might want to hold onto these." I gave her the papers drawn up the night before. "Dr. Josiah Simons, the new Superintendent of Hudson is the man to thank."

"Dr. Joey? Oh, there will be marvellous changes. You are a magician, professor!" Another Marcello hug was wrapped around me, and I reciprocated in kind.

"Miss Marcello, there is one more thing. I have arranged for a scholarship for your niece at Vassar College. She can test now and begin in the fall. Vassar will focus her supreme intelligence toward the science she chooses to study. Please contact President Taylor who has been apprised."

"Wonderful, professor, thank you."

I waved her off. "I advise you to put your things in order. We leave immediately."

"I'm going to Vassar this year? Hooray! Aunt Rita, I'll help you." And they left.

"When is your ship sailing—murder?" Mrs. Stanton said.

I opened my watch. "It leaves in two hours. The Superintendent of Hudson Asylum killed a patient in cold blood, he was caught red-handed. Thanks to Miss Rita's quick thinking, the Poughkeepsie authorities have enough proof to put an end to his horrific dominion."

Mrs. Stanton studied me for a moment. "Yesterday's affair was such a success all round. My dear friend, Susan, rescued 13 women and 10 children from that horrible asylum."

"Do you know if they are well-provisioned and traveling north?" I said.

"Yes and the houses were happy to host them. Miss Tubman was delighted to join in the fun. What an extraordinary event. It was a pleasure working with you."

"A singular and most illuminating occurrence."

"So, Professor Feathers, how have you fared since your liberation?"

"Gratefully, all the difficulty was left behind at the moment of my conversion. I find the antithesis of prejudice reconciles well with my personal pursuits. Thanks to your and Miss Anthony's achievements, the young women at Vassar College will continue to establish a new direction for this country. The college encourages such freedom and the child will do well there. With your tutelage, she is sure to blossom."

"As my daughter has. Looking through the lens of the Temperance Movement who would think that a brewer could create something as wonderful as the first actual college for women in this country? Vassar was a working-class man of vision. Brilliance does not brook class distinctions and sprouts even in the humblest gardens.

But I wonder why you are forgoing your role in Rachel's destiny?" She nodded her head in the girl's direction.

Miss Rita and the child joined us with her luggage.

The doorbell rang. It was Marcello with our carriage.

"It's time to go. Let's not keep Marcello waiting."

"Generous Mrs. Stanton, thank you for sharing your wonderful home with me, I'll visit right after my California trip, and tell you all about it." Miss Rita said.

"My pleasure, Miss Marcello, and please bring back to me the western suffrage news. Miss Rachel, do visit me frequently. Professor, be careful on your steamship home. People feel freer on a ship out to sea. With your change of heart you may wind up engaged."

"Mrs. Stanton." I knelt. "My heart belongs to one woman only." I kissed her hand.

"My valiant, 'Feathers." She smiled, raised me up and gave me her card. "Call or cable me as soon as you're able. And send me the British suffragist news. The rumours I hear are worrisome."

CHAPTER 24
AN ENTIRELY CONNECTED CASE

"But I could not rest, Watson, I could not sit quiet in my chair, if I thought that such a man as Professor Moriarty were walking the streets of London unchallenged."–Dr. John H. Watson. "The Adventure of the Final Problem."

My dear Watson,

My steamship leaves port today. I will reach London by Thursday, March 29th with no plans for the Fool's Day, except dining with you at Marcini's on Mycroft's tab.

After my adventures, I only hope to see your welcoming face and hear that voice which has always been so full of the questions that has completed me and my searches for justice. This trip has unlocked so many of my closed doors. I wonder will you recognize me, dear boy.

There is one evildoer who impatiently awaits my return and I am supremely prepared for him. The trap will be carefully baited, the hunter will not be able to resist, and we will pounce!

As you know me to be, dear partner,

Very sincerely yours,

S. H.

Marcello, Miss Rita, the child, and I travelled by carriage downtown, with the Hudson River on our right. Our destination: Pier 40 on Clarkson Street. The good ship *Lucania*, Cunard Line, bound for Liverpool was docked and waiting.

"Now, with your permission, I will demonstrate the simple sequence of events that led to your complicated rescue, Miss Marcello."

"Thank you, professor."

"First, your whereabouts, following her persistent proclaiming of your dire situation I escorted your niece to every local authority. No result was ascertained. A chance interview substantiated by Harold's barbershop gossip revealed Pinto was newly single, but not divorced, selling his home, but not leaving Poughkeepsie. Yet he was clearly attempting to raise fast funds. The balance of probability was that Miss Rita had been cast aside but was alive in some uncommon place. I concluded that only through Pinto was forward momentum possible."

"You chose the most dangerous way, why didn't you just talk to Shawn Reilly?" Marcello said.

"Still concerned for my safety, Marcello?" I smiled at him. "Pinto is not so foolish; he positioned himself at Reilly's back so his information was irrelevant. With your and Miss Marietta's helpful counsel, I naturally began by examining the house. And found proof of Miss Rita's commitment and the annulment of their marriage. My telegram to Hudson confirmed it." I patted her hand.

"Second, your release, I realized the complexity in venturing a successful rescue if our legal plans broke down and commenced my search for accomplished collaboration. Miss Marietta devised a plan to incorporate your family and staged visits to support you through the lengthy legal process."

"What a delight to have such a scheming and intelligent sister at my back." Miss Rita said.

"She is a singular and most generous lady. During our mock-birthday visitation your brother, Felice, wanted to take them on then and there. His courage shone in that dank and dreary place, as he restored our ability to confer without being overheard. I am curious, how did you fare that day, Miss Marcello?"

"No punishment and my meal restrictions were removed."

"Then our involvement achieved its purpose that day. Dr. Philips was contracted by the child and myself. Your niece would make a fine comic actress, if she weren't such a true hearted scientist." She looked up at me with a smile. "As we unfortunately established, consignment to Hudson Asylum is easily achieved, and the action of the lowest form of human. If the need arises, know that Philips is a superb and kind professional. He recommended Morris Henry's legal advice. Both men laid out the requirements for your sanity hearing. This set the family up for your trial.

"The child and I then involved Mrs. Stanton and Miss Anthony who devised an ingenious addition to the rescue, and made it look like an outing in the park. Further the impromptu chaos created by the suffragists allowed us the moments we needed for our skilful escape on the ice. The women and children these ladies welcomed into their march will shortly be embarking on new lives in the British Dominion of Canada." I nodded to him. "Marcello involved Houdini, who with the assistance of Nurse Nancy and Dr. Josiah, kept the staff occupied and then put them to sleep, probably not going on any of Houdini's posters. Ha!"

The cab slowed and the cabbie interrupted us. "'Scuse me, sir, we are ordered to stop. It's the p'lice." He reined in his horses. Two very young policemen representing New York City's Finest were stamping their feet at a temporary boundary, and asked us to identify ourselves.

Marcello confronted them. "What is this about?" Miss Rita took his hand, shook her head, and smiled at him.

"There's escaped lunatics from upriver, da whole force is lookin' for 'em." We calmly introduced ourselves, including Miss Rita's alias. They asked Mr. Sigerson to get out. I hopped down, shook hands and signed autographs. Then lit a cigarette and offered them to the officers. I nonchalantly mentioned my steamship and in a matter of minutes they let us go. *"Arrivederci!"*

We were again underway. "Miss Rita, you have confounded the entire New York City Police Force."

"Rita—how?" Marcello said.

"Oh, Miss Anthony is very thorough. She prepared me for this situation." Miss Rita brought out her new passport. "And call me Sally!" We laughed.

"Professor Sigerson, please continue." The child said.

I smiled. "My undercover exploration of the asylum garnered important clues as to the identity of this potent authority." Six sets of eyes were glued to my every word. "As far as that ersatz trial, it was clear the cards were stacked against you, so we opted for our intriguingly quick escape. I am grateful, Marcello, for your swift and professional inauguration of our plans. Dr. Josiah informed me that the wires were cut so competently, his man easily restored communications."

"I knew if I enlisted those who had a history of success in such matters and added to it the dynamic ability to mesmerize an audience, plus the courage to walk into the asylum with loaded guns, that the rescue would be achieved." I doused my cigarette and shook Marcello's hand. "Such powerful deceptions on six consecutive stages, allowed us to escape onward to Mrs. Stanton's home by virtue of Miss Rita's exceptional ice yacht skills." I patted her hand. "Just when we thought all was lost some surprisingly arresting and dangerous heroics by Mr. Paulo Marcello and his niece allowed us to continue to New York." I shook her hand.

The child smiled. "There was no danger; when out on the ice, the Commodore's orders are followed without question by all members of the yacht club. I had the tough job; do you have any idea how difficult it is to keep two flags visible in that wind?" We laughed as our horse's hooves clattered down the west side.

Marcello said. "Overnight, Albert taught Marietta how to handle a gun, we didn't have much time, but at close range how could she miss?"

"With the asylum's secrets, and strange therapies, I felt in my bones a central force at work. Events proved that I had judged correctly. As an orderly, I uncovered and brought them each into my confidence. It would be the Simons' brothers, Lacassio or Edwards. They surely had motive and ability. I knew they were capable of anything. I watched them, Marcello, but fell into their trap, instead."

"Yeah, and if we had gotten there any later, you'd still be there, as either a eunuch or a vegetable." Marcello said. I looked at him and we burst out into a fit of laughter. I patted his back and lit us both a cigarette.

"Thank God you did, Uncle Oscar."

"Third, the murder, As we hurtled south via the train which completed our great ice yacht escape, Miss Rita courageously disclosed to me the murder she had been forced to witness the night before." I looked in her eyes and took her hand. "I flew back to the asylum and with Dr. Josiah's help, conducted a detailed investigation of the scene." I patted her hand. "Because of your courage and supreme mind, Miss Marcello, this murder caught up with Simons. Here is today's *Poughkeepsie Daily Eagle*. With his predilection for electrical murder is it not too absurd to suppose that the electric chair may be an appropriate punishment?"

"Supreme mind, I'm glad to hear that from a gentleman." Miss Rita smiled as she read the paper.

"I obtained enough evidence to convict him, and your testimony in the witness box would strengthen it, but that is your privilege. If you are so moved, speak with Mr. Henry."

"I have always laid great stress upon reasoning from trifles the larger image, and much practice has made it second nature to me. I discovered circumstances which validated your story. And in Simons' office, a gloating confession was left behind as an impression on his desk blotter. I had Helena's map which delineated the unmarked graves exactly where the bodies were located. When the police dug up the lawn, they found more than one corpse. Mr. Battaglia's wounds exactly matched your description.

"After presenting Simons with the facts, I interviewed him. He disclosed enough to corroborate his damning narrative. I consolidated the evidence and put it in Mr. Henry's capable hands, along with a signed statement of my findings. He has the means to successfully prosecute Simons for deliberate, premeditated, cold-blooded murder."

The child shook my hand. "But, Professor Sigerson, don't you need to be here for the trial?"

"Ah, child, 'Thrice is he armed who hath his quarrel just.' I am confident that Mr. Henry can bring this to fruition without me. Never fear, I have given him all the ammunition he needs. It is essential that I leave today".

"I might have a conversation with Dr. Josiah about his plans." Miss Rita said.

"I'm sure he'd welcome that."

We arrived at the pier. "Come aboard for a tour, it is precisely the ship from my first trip. Not in crew quarters this time."

I had returned to my strength and was departing the States to fulfil my destiny in London. We jumped from the cab; I escorted the child up the gangplank behind arriving luggage and passengers. We secured my luggage in the on-deck stateroom. The girl said, wide-eyed. "This is a boat?" Wood panelled, thickly carpeted. Velvet curtains, richly upholstered furniture. "Look at all this room!"

"When it's time to hop over for a visit, you and your Uncle Oscar will enjoy your own stateroom."

"I wish it was now."

When Marcello joined us, she was crying into my handkerchief.

"Rachel, you must see the dance hall. It's filled with mermaids, and there are at least a thousand people saying farewell, waving handkerchiefs, and a *New York Times* photographer, you don't want to miss this." Marcello said.

We exited to the main deck, into the sky-lit dining saloon. The domed skylight ceiling was made of blue and gold stained glass mermaids. The wood-panelled walls had decoratively carved classical mermaids in white and gold.

"The morning and evening light transforms it. This is where I fiddled my way across. And I will do so again. Marcello, what are your plans?"

"We go from here to meet a friend of Rachel's, and now Rita can join them on a train back to Poughkeepsie. Following that, my compatriots and I take the transcontinental express across the country for final fair set-up. It should take just four days to put us at the West Coast."

Miss Rita said. "You know, Oscar, I just might join you."

"Aunt Marietta has a trip to the fair already planned, Aunt Rita, and she hoped you would join her." The child said.

"I'm sure she'd rather the professor joined her."

Miss Marietta's intelligent and resourceful gentleness will be missed. I admired these young Marcello's, yet, I was eager for an eminent London adventure with my ever faithful Watson. Marcello and Miss Rita said farewell and left the ship, giving the child her chance to say goodbye.

From the pier they watched open-mouthed, as a young man ran up through the crowds of people moving on the gangplank. Upon reaching the deck he turned, aimed at me and fired off a shot which whizzed past the child. The sound of the shot echoed off the Cunard Line Building and created intense perturbation as the frenzied passengers flew into the dining saloon. I launched the child with a compelling shove. "Go to the cabin, NOW!" The ship's bell rang and a confusion of people ran down the gangplank, scattering as fast as they could. In an instant, the deck was empty except for the assassin and me. He raised his gun, I growled, leapt to him and knocked it out of his hand with my stick, and the force of it propelled it over the side.

The assassin drove me to the railing. I gained my feet and pinned him. "What is your name, boy?"

He pulled away from me and sneered. "James Moriarty!"

In my rage and anger at Rachel's endangerment, I smashed my fist into his jaw, then before he had a chance to raise his hands I dazed him with a solid right uppercut. He shook his head and counterpunched attempting a one, two combination, I parried his right and his second jab hit me in the solar plexus with a weak left. I smiled and in quick succession slammed my powerful left into his jaw once, then twice, the third was the haymaker, he fell to the deck. I held my gun to his head, and cocked it. "Son, I have dispatched 30 of your kind and you are lucky to be alive, do not tempt me."

The crew secured and brought him to the brig and I was taken to the Captain's great chart room. "Please forgive my delaying your departure, Captain McKay." I saluted him.

"Mr. Holmes?"

"Yes sir."

"I've already wired the New York Police Department. With luck, we'll be off in a couple of hours. Your fight will be the talk of the ship, I opened the bar early, passengers are already celebrating.

"Thank you, sir.

"Mr. Holmes, tell me all you know of the man you subdued on my deck."

"He is an assassin out for me, not well skilled, and said his name was James Moriarty. I have fought many like him on the continent, yet I did not expect to find one here."

McKay said. "He discharged his pistol on my deck. He was lucky to face you. I would have shot him. The safety of my ship and protection of a full roster of passengers was at stake. You are a hero."

"Be that as it may, what do you think the Police Department will do with me?"

"Nothing, I imagine, once I make it clear to them that this ruffian has threatened my passengers at gunpoint and held up my voyage. And that you, a crewman stepped up and saved the day, saved his life as I was readying to shoot him. Say nothing of assassins or that he was after you personally. I will fully cooperate with them, as will you, yet I can only grant them a couple of hours to accomplish their task. But there is nothing to worry about." I saluted him.

A crewman entered the cabin. "Captain, the police have arrived." He handed McKay a two stripe Cunard line uniform.

"Thank you mate, lower the gangplank and bring them on board. Mr. Holmes, your uniform, I will refer to you as Mate Newton?"

"Yes sir."

We met with New York City Police Inspector Crowley and four officers. They handcuffed and brought their man from the brig into their waiting black growler. The inspector interviewed Captain McKay and me. I admired the captain's equanimity under fire; he was a courteous host and had made it easy for the police. His chef brought fresh coffee and breakfast comestibles. When I came on deck to detail the scene, the passengers cheered, underlining my story. The inspector was satisfied with our account and the captain would be back in New York in two weeks if needed. The Police Inspector gave the order to shove off. The gangplank was raised, the whistle blew, and the *Lucania* left port, an hour and a half later than expected. I shook hands with Captain McKay and left his cabin.

The boy who attempted to kill me was secured in a New York gaol; the ship passengers were celebrating Easter a day early, and the girl was still in my cabin. I ran to her side.

She said. "You're alright?" She hugged me tightly. "Thank God! I've been praying for you."

I looked down at her and began to breathe again. "Intelligence and sensibility, a rare pairing, I am proud of you. Come with me child, we need to send a message." I took her by the hand and we ran to the stern. We had seconds to mime a message to Marcello and Miss Rita who had remained with the throng of gawkers on shore. Then sprinted to the communications room to send telegrams before the ship moved out of range. One to the Marcello family and to Oscar Marcello's Manhattan studio to say I would keep the child safe.

The *Lucania* headed for the open with one remarkably unexpected passenger aboard. The ship travelled majestically downriver, tugboats fore and aft, through that churned and swirled conjunction where the sumptuous Hudson in its final beneficence poured itself out into New York Harbour. As if requesting her blessing, the ship gave a whistle to *La Liberté éclairant le monde*.

We returned to the stateroom. I sat cross-legged in a chair, lit a cigarette and considered the girl before me. "Miss Rachel, it appears you will realize your wish to rendezvous with Dr. John Watson. He is my friend and colleague and I am Sherlock Holmes."

She smiled. "Aw, I knew that when we met on Market Street."

All across the crowded harbour, *Lucania's* whistle was heard greeting each vessel from tug to ferry, steamship to tall-masted schooner. Then she purposefully moved out to sea.

The End

ACKNOWLEDGEMENTS

To those who abhor the dull routine of existence, and who choose instead to analyse the abstruse and intricate predicaments offered in the pages of a mystery. I salute you!

The writer's process is unique, but not so unique to other like-minded creatives, scientists, artists, musicians, performers and illusionists. We all know a like cultivation of our mind and powers and the life-affirming desire to use the almighty tool of language to bring a sort of justice into the world.

This book is homage to the ever-present spirit of Sherlock Holmes and the thrill shared in anticipation of the as yet unsolved problem. Dr. Joe Bell, the generous, loving, wise and spectacularly gifted man of science who was also, some say, the inspiration for Sherlock Holmes. After Doyle, one must always discover Bell. Jeremy Brett, whose definitive portrayal and supreme dedication, awakened us all to the essence and humour of Sir Arthur Conan Doyle's stories. David Burke's ground-breaking depiction of one of the two definitive Dr. Watson's for Granada TV and Edward Hardwicke in life and on stage a best friend in the true spirit of Dr. John H. Watson.

J. R. Altabef we both rose like phoenix and ventured onto the road less travelled, your courage, compassion, and true musical genius are ever my inspiration. Pamela Josephine Russo always my persistent and gentle cheerleader. Bud Bruskewicz went beyond Mycroft, to dirty his hands with this book. Rob Sturgeon saved me from ennui. My parents, who saw the truth and protected me from it.

Steven Emecz, a modern day visionary to empower us all. Gimone Hall, compassionate, accomplished and much missed mentor. B. Gail Cooper, my incomparable editor. Vassar College

Historian, Colton Johnson's time machine graciously transported me to 1894. The ardent and generous Catherine Cooke, librarian in charge of the Westminster Research Library, and the Sherlock Holmes Collection, London. David Marcum's astute Canonical wisdom, led me ever onward. Friends and family who shared the wisdom only accomplished practitioners would know and encouraged this process along the way: Christine Bush, Paula Clinchy, Elizabeth Crowens, Gary Culp, Darlene Cypser, Susan Dahlinger, Sue Davies, Nieves Fernandez, Susan Manning, Lutz Muller, Dore Nash, Lindy Rogers, Robin Rowles, Mark Sohn, Maureen Whittaker, and Andy Wright. The world-wide Sherlockian, Holmesian, Watsonian, and Doylean Community: Most especially, the Sherlock Holmes Society of London, my home away from home, the John H. Watson Society, and New York's Adventuresses of Sherlock Holmes.

Sir Arthur Conan Doyle, whose genius and artistry brought these exceptional stories into our hearts where Sherlock Holmes, Dr. Watson, and you, Sir Arthur, live forever.

EPILOGUE
FINAL REVEAL

This story is an attempt to bring to a close a cloaked horror buried deep in the past, based on the life of an ancestor. Her story the scaffolding onto which this pastiche is mounted. Like me, she was an intelligent woman who spoke her mind. On her cruel and violent husband's word alone, she was committed to an asylum. She spent forty years in the Hudson River State Hospital, in medically prescribed and state-sanctioned captivity.

"Sherlock Holmes: These Scattered Houses" is a child's rescue fantasy. This secret has haunted me since it's unmasking in my youth. Through the gracious intercession of Mr. Sherlock Holmes, the mystery has now been put to rest.

SELECTED BIBLOGRAPHY

Prologue
1. "Bradshaw's Handbook 1861." London: HarperCollins, 2014 (originally published as Bradshaw's Descriptive Railway Hand-Book of Great Britain and Ireland 1861).
2. Moss, Stephen. "Why Wagner's Tristan und Isolde is the ultimate opera." London: *The Guardian*. 23 Sep 2016
3. Bell, Dr Joseph. "A Manual of the Operations of Surgery." Alberta, Canada: Okitoks Press, 2017 (originally published, Edinburgh: Oliver and Boyd, 1892.) Master Surgeon and distinguished professor of medicine at the University of Edinburgh, President of the Royal College of Surgeons of Edinburgh, and personal surgeon to Queen Victoria. He was Arthur Conan Doyle's inspiration for Sherlock Holmes.

Chapter 1
4. Research excursions to Vassar College and a visit with Vassar College Historian Colton Johnson. Notes from personal interviews and investigations of 1894 Vassar College. March 2019, Poughkeepsie, New York.
5. "Vassar College Digital Library." 1894 Historical references: Vassar President Taylor's papers, about the student body, teachers, subjects, layout, rooms, general history, et al. https://digitallibrary.vassar.edu/collections/earlyvassar

Chapter 2
6. I owe most of this chapter to Holmes astute musical ear and a violinist friend of mine.

Chapter 3
7. Farnham, Charles H. "Ice Yachting on the Hudson." *Scribner's Monthly.* 1881.
8. Watson, Dr. John H. "The Man with the Twisted Lip." Quote.

Chapter 4
9. Three quotes by Harry Houdini. "Wild About Harry." A well-researched and updated Houdini website created by John Cox: https://www.wildabouthoudini.com/

Chapter 5
10. "Vassar Encyclopaedia." 1894 Historical references: Student journals, letters, photographs, chronology of events, telephone, heating, trolley, et al. http://vcencyclopedia.vassar.edu/index.html
11. Benson Lossing. "Vassar College and Its Founder." Historian and founding trustee of Vassar College. 1867.

Chapter 6
12. Research excursions to Poughkeepsie, New York. The old city. Uncovered, mapped, reimagined and trekked the historic streets, hills, houses, Hudson River State Hospital, Bardavon Opera House, factories, and businesses of 1894 Poughkeepsie and its famed Hudson River vistas. 2018 and 2019.

Chapter 7
13. Houdini, Harry. "The Right Way to Do Wrong." New York: Amereon House. 2011 (first published 1906).

Chapter 8
14. Three quotes by Samuel Morse. "Letter 1855." "What hath God wrought?" The first telegraphed message sent by Morse, May 24, 1844.

15. Note 1: Please forgive my only anachronistic misrepresentation of time. Samuel Morse officially died April 2, 1872.
16. Note 2: To be precise, while in New York, the American "second floor" was referenced. Yet, to all British subjects, it was actually the "first floor." This distinction was carried throughout.

Chapter 9

17. Salmon, Andrew. "Queensberry Justice: The Fight Card Sherlock Holmes Omnibus." Fight Card Books, 2016.
18. "The Victorian Gentleman's Self-Defence Toolkit Part II." https://outofthiscentury.wordpress.com/2015/03/16/the-victorian-gentlemans-self-defense-toolkit-part-ii/
19. McKay, Brett and McKay, Kate. "Manly Slang from the 19th Century." 2010. Updated: 2017. https://www.artofmanliness.com/articles/manly-slang-from-the-19th-century/

Chapter 10

20. "New York Legislative Documents, Volume 19." Section 1146-A Of The Civil Practice Act of An Action for Annulment of a Marriage. 1938. 49-51.

Chapter 11

21. Watson, Dr. John H. "The Sign of Four." Quote.

Chapter 12

22. Lathrop, Caldwell Clarissa. "A Secret Institution." Gilbert, Arizona: Endeavour Compass, 2018 (originally published 1892.) Lathrop's autobiography described her confinement at the New York State Lunatic Asylum at Utica. Praised for exposing 19th-century mental institutions, and how outspoken

women were confined. She fought to be moved to Hudson River State Hospital where her sanity was tested and established.

Chapter 13

23. Bly, Nellie. "Ten Days in a Madhouse." New York: Norman L. Munro, 1887. Newspaper reporter Nellie Bly published a series of articles for the *New York World* newspaper. She was committed to an insane asylum while on undercover assignment, where she investigated the brutality and neglect at Blackwell's Island Women's Asylum. This prompted a grand jury investigation with Bly assisting. New York added a million dollars more per year for the care of the insane and carried out her recommendations.

24. "Quando il gioco e finite, il re e il pedone vanno nella stessa scatola." Translation: After the game, the king and the pawn go into the same box. An Italian Proverb.

Chapter 14

25. Dix, Dorothea. "I Tell What I Have Seen–The Reports of Asylum Reformer Dorothea Dix. Excerpted from Memorial to the Legislature of Massachusetts. Boston." Munroe & Francis, 1843.

Chapter 15

26. Dubois, Ellen Carol, Editor. "Elizabeth Cady Stanton, Susan B. Anthony: Correspondence, Writings, Speeches." New York: Schocken Books, 1981. Two quotes by Elizabeth Cady Stanton, excerpted from her "Seneca Falls Keynote Address," July 19, 1848.

27. Shakespeare, William. "Henry V," Act III. Quote. "The Complete Works of William Shakespeare." http://shakespeare.mit.edu/
28. Guy, Particia, Kalson, Katherine, editors. "Ladies, Ladies: The Women in the Life of Sherlock Holmes." New York: Aventine Press, 2007.
29. Note 3: Uncle Fred's Nose, This Vassar College building was completed in 1893 (The Fredrick Ferris Thompson Annex.) The library was a three-story annex, extending from the front of Main, included a porte-cochere built out of veined white marble, which served as the remodelled entrance to Vassar. A student in 1893 asserts: "Proved a most delightful place for study, was admirably lighted and ventilated, and its alcoves were attractive."
30. Watson, Dr. John H. "The Man with the Twisted Lip." Quote.

Chapter 16

31. Thucydides. Quote. Ancient Greek historian and author, 460-404bc. "The bravest are surely those who have the clearest vision of what is before them, glory and danger alike, and yet notwithstanding go out to meet it."

Chapter 17

32. Hecato of Rhodes, a Greek Stoic philosopher, "Si vis amari, ama." Translation: To be loved, love. 100 BC

Chapter 18

33. Packard, Elizabeth. "The Prisoner's Hidden Life or Insane Asylums Unveiled." Montana: Kessinger Publishing, 2008 (originally published 1868). 1816-1897. She was consigned to the Jacksonville, Illinois Insane Asylum, by her husband, from

1860 to 1863. She spent the rest of her life working to ameliorate conditions in asylums.
34. Galton, Francis F.R. "Inquieies Into Human Faculty And Its Development." New York: Macmillan and Company, 1883. He coined the term, "Eugenics."
35. Wallis, Jennifer. "This fascinating and fatal disease: The History of 'General Paralysis of the Insane' in the Victorian Asylum." *The Psychologist*, Magazine of the British Psychological Society: October 2012. An historical study of syphilis and its psychological effects.
36. Bucknill, John Charles and Tuke, Daniel Hack. "A Manual of Psychological Medicine: Insanity." Exciting or Determining Causes of Insanity. Philadelphia: P. Blakiston, Son & Co, 1879.

Chapter 19
37. Martin, David C. "Clinical Methods: The History, Physical, and Laboratory Examinations. The Mental Status Examination." Oxford: Butterworth Publishers, 1990. There were many more questions to the Test for Lunacy, which for brevity's sake were ignored, in this chapter.
38. Hammond, William A. "The Treatment Of The Insane." The Utica Crib. The International Review, Volume VIII. New York: Barnes & Company, March 1880.
39. Cicero, Marcus Tullius. Roman statesman, orator, lawyer and philosopher, who served as consul in the year 63 BC. "Amicitiae nostrae memoriam spero sempiternam fore." Translation: I hope that the memory of our friendship will be everlasting.

Chapter 20

40. "Annual report of the New York State Commission in Lunacy for the year 1889." http://www.archive.org/stream/annualreportsta110unkngoog/annualreportsta110unkngoog_djvu.txt

Chapter 21

41. Thompson, Francis. "The Hound of Heaven." Poem. 1859-1907.
42. Watson, Dr. John H. "A Study in Scarlet." Quote.

Chapter 22

43. "Hudson River State Hospital: Fourteen Decades of Mental Hygiene." https://sometimes-interesting.com/2016/01/27/hudson-river-state-hospital-fourteen-decades-of-mental-hygiene/#pilgrim

Chapter 23

44. Dubois, Ellen Carol, Editor. "Elizabeth Cady Stanton, Susan B. Anthony: Correspondence, Writings, Speeches." "The Solitude of Self." Farewell speech to the National Woman Suffrage Association, 1892. New York: Schocken Books, 1981.
45. Watson, Dr. John H. "The Adventure of the Naval Treaty." Quote.

Chapter 24

46. Shakespeare, William. "Henry IV." Part 2 act III. Quote.
47. "La Liberté éclairant le monde." Translation: Liberty Enlightening the World.

WORKS USED THROUGHOUT

48. Doyle, Sir Arthur Conan. "The Complete Sherlock Holmes. Volume I and II." New York: Doubleday.
49. Baring-Gold, William. "The Annotated Sherlock Holmes." New York: Clarkson N. Potter, 1967.
50. Kilinger, Leslie. "New Annotated Sherlock Holmes." New York: W.W. Norton & Company, 2005.
51. Doyle, Sir Arthur Conan. "The Original Illustrated 'Strand' Sherlock Holmes." Hertfordshire, UK: Wordsworth Editions, 1989.
52. Doyle, Sir Arthur Conan. "The Complete Sherlock Holmes Treasury." New York: Crown Publishers, 1975.
53. Doyle, Sir Arthur Conan. "The Final Adventures of Sherlock Holmes." New York: Warner Books, 1981.
54. Knox, Monsignor Ronald A. "Studies in the Literature of Sherlock Holmes-1st Paper". Oxford, UK: Presented to the Gryphon Club in 1911. Published in The Blue Book Magazine, 1912.
55. Hicks, Seymour Brookfield, Charles, Hallam Elton. "Under the Clock," London: 1893. This first Sherlock Holmes Parody. Written by Hicks was staged at the Royal Court Theatre, London, during Holmes "Great Hiatus." A copy of original read at the Westminster Research Library, Sherlock Holmes Collection. Catherine Cooke, Managing Librarian.
56. Liebow, Ely M. "Dr Joe Bell, Model for Sherlock Holmes." Madison, Wisconsin: Popular Press, 2007 (original publication1982.)

57. Marcum, David, Editor. "Holmes Away From Home. Adventures From The Great Hiatus. Volume Two 1893 – 1894." Manchester, NH: Belanger Books, 2016.
58. Kurkland, Michael, Editor. "Sherlock Holmes The Hidden Years." New York: Minotaur Books, 2004.
59. Blackbeard, Bill. Sherlock Holmes in America. New York: Harry N. Abrams, Inc. 1981.
60. Weller, Philip. "The Life and Times of Sherlock Holmes." London: Bracken Books, 1993.
61. Bostrom, Mattias. "From Holmes to Sherlock." New York: Mysterious Press, 2017.
62. Paul, Jeremy, Brett, Jeremy. "The Secret of Sherlock Holmes." Los Angeles: Players Press, Inc. 1989.
63. Doyle, Sir Arthur Conan and Gillette, William. "Sherlock Holmes." A play in two acts. New York: Samuel French, 1976, (originally produced on Broadway in 1899.)
64. "The Arthur Conan Doyle Encyclopaedia." Maintained by Alexis Barquin:
   https://www.arthur-conan-doyle.com/index.php/Sherlock_Holmes/
65. Cox, Michael. "A Study in Celluloid: A Producer's Account of Jeremy Brett as Sherlock Holmes." Cambridge, UK: Rupert Books, 1999.
66. Rathbone, Basil. "In and Out of Character." Autobiography. New York: Limelight Editions, 2004 (first published 1956).
67. The Granada Television Series, "Sherlock Holmes." Jeremy Brett, David Burke, and Edward Hardwicke. The series ran from 1984- 1994. Forty-one films based on Sir Arthur Conan Doyle's stories.

68. "Lost in Limehouse." 1933 burlesque by the Masquers for RKO Release.
69. Sherlock Holmes Portrayals on Film, TV and Theatre: Jeremy Brett, Ronald Howard, Ellie Norwood, John Barrymore, Sir Robert Stephens, Ian Richardson, William Gillette, Vasily Livanov, Christopher Plummer, Igor Petrenko, Sir Ian McKellen, Douglas Wilmer, Basil Rathbone, Ben Kingsley, Georges Treville, Arthur Wontner, Christopher Lee, Alan Napier, John Cleese, Benedict Cumberbatch, Robert Downey Jr., Peter Cushing, Sir Michael Caine, Gene Wilder, and Basil of Baker Street.
70. Stanton, Elizabeth Cady. "Elizabeth Cady Stanton as revealed in her letters, diary and reminiscences, 1815-1902." New York and London: Harper & brothers, 1932.
71. Stanton, Elizabeth Cady, Anthony, Susan Brownell. "The Selected Papers of Elizabeth Cady Stanton and Susan B. Anthony: When clowns make laws for queens, 1880-1887." New Jersey: Rutgers University Press, 2006.
72. Stanton, Elizabeth Cady. "Eighty Years and More: Reminiscences, 1815-1897." Boston: Northeastern University Press, 1993 (originally published 1898).
73. Stanton, Elizabeth Cady, Anthony, Susan Brownell. "History of Woman Suffrage: 1883-1900." New York: J. J. Little & Ives Company, 1922.

Cover painting: Henry Gritten (British/Australian, 1818-1873). *Springside: View of Gardener's Cottage and Barns*, 1852. Oil on canvas. Frances Lehman Loeb Art Center, Vassar College, Poughkeepsie, New York, gift of Thomas M. Evans, Jr., in honor of Tania Goss, class of 1959, 2015.22.1.

Lightning Source UK Ltd.
Milton Keynes UK
UKHW020626141221
395640UK00011B/800